SUBMITTING TO THE COWBOY

Cowboy Doms Book Three

BJ WANE

Published by Blushing Books
An Imprint of
ABCD Graphics and Design, Inc.
A Virginia Corporation
977 Seminole Trail #233
Charlottesville, VA 22901

BJ Wane
Submitting to the Cowboy

EBook ISBN: 978-1-64563-004-3
Print ISBN: 978-1-64563-036-4
v1

Cover Art by ABCD Graphics & Design

Chapter 1

Reaching for the door handle, Connor Dunbar winced at the twinge of pain radiating from front to back in his shoulder. The surgery he had undergone to repair the damaged muscles from a bullet wound left him aching; the weakness frustrated him. Entering The Barn, a private BDSM club he owned with his brother, Caden and Sheriff Grayson Monroe, he admitted the fault for the injury he'd sustained over six weeks ago lay solely on his shoulders. He hadn't needed the stupidity of chasing after a truck of cattle rustlers alone drilled into him by his brother, as well as others. He'd come to that conclusion all by himself as he'd driven back to his house, injured, in the middle of the night.

From the number of shoes filling the cubbies along one wall of the foyer leading into the renovated barn, it looked like another well-attended Friday night of kinky play was in progress. The coat closet held a few jackets, but as usual, March in Central Montana had roared in like a lion, dumping several feet of snow only to follow a scant week later with temperatures in the low fifties that had encouraged people to come out without their heavy winter gear. Using his good arm, he opened the door leading into the playroom, the snap of leather striking bare skin a welcome sound after his absence the past few weeks.

Pausing, Connor took a moment to breathe in the enticing scent of hay bales stacked along one wall, providing a perch or ledge to position a sub and the subtle odor of sex mingling with leather. Scanning the crowd, he found Caden behind the bar in the center of the room, his fiancée, Sydney seated on a stool next to Avery, Grayson's new girl. Since the sheriff wasn't glued to her side, Connor guessed he was monitoring the loft activity where they'd positioned most of the bondage equipment. Looking up, he spotted Sue Ellen bound at a chain station, her sweat-slick body swaying as her husband, Master Brett wielded a crop on her delectable ass. Her shrill cry reverberated down and drew his smile. Damn, but he'd missed this place.

His head had been up his ass for weeks before he'd made the blunder of chasing criminals without even informing anyone of his solo stakeout. The pain and weakness resulting from that idiocy had forced him to get his act together. The problem was, he honestly didn't know why he'd been out of sorts. His attitude tumble had started last fall, but the reason for it still eluded him. His friends thought it was due to his break-up with Annie, whom he'd been enjoying a six-month, monogamous relationship with until he'd discovered her infidelity. But the truth was, he'd been distracted and irritable before he'd walked in on her and her vanilla lover.

With a sigh, Connor shoved aside unanswered questions and vowed to enjoy himself tonight. Winding his way through the seating area between the doors and bar, he stopped at a table to say hello to Dan Shylock, a long-time friend and popular Dom among the subs. Curled on the lawyer's lap, the disheveled, red-faced brunette sporting clamped nipples and a G-string appeared glassy-eyed and well-used.

"A little early to have someone already enjoying subspace, isn't it?" Connor winked at the girl whose name eluded him.

Dan smiled. "Never too early. Good to see you back. How's the shoulder?" The concern clouding his dark eyes both irritated and warmed Connor.

Shaking his head, he nudged his Stetson back with a thumb, drawling, "Don't you and Caden ever get tired of playing mother hen? I had to suffer through two weeks of that from my own mother after surgery. Give me a break, will you?"

"Yeah, okay, you're right. But I can't speak for your brother." Dan inclined his blond head toward the bar where Connor saw Caden watching him with a careful eye.

Stifling the urge to roll his eyes, Connor glanced back down at Dan's play partner and suddenly recalled her name. "Stacy, right?" At her slow nod and gleam of interest in her blue eyes, he smiled. "When you've recovered and are ready to move on from this brute, come look me up, sweetie. I'm much nicer than he is."

Dan's rude snort followed him as he strode to the bar and slid onto a stool next to Sydney. Tugging on her long red hair, he winked at the girl who had snagged his brother in just a few short weeks of hiring on at their ranch as the new cook. "I'm here. Happy now?" Out of all his well-meaning friends, her nagging concern had touched him the most. The assistance he'd given her in getting Caden to open his eyes to a relationship with an employee had forged a special bond between the two of them.

A beaming smile lit up her green eyes. "Yes, and you look good. Better than you have in weeks."

"Gee, thanks," he returned dryly, quirking one brow.

"And now that you do, she can return to giving me her undivided attention," Caden said, setting a draft in front of Connor. "Do you want to spell Grayson upstairs for an hour now or do you have plans?"

It was just like his brother to hide his relief and pleasure at Connor's presence after the weeks of convalescing by getting right down to business. "I'm good with now." Leaning around Sydney, he smiled at Avery. "I wouldn't want to keep you waiting, sweetie. Not after you set up the new laptop you recommended for me. I would have gone bonkers if I hadn't been able to play my games while I was being good obeying doctor's orders."

This time, the rude, disbelieving snorts came from all three of them before Avery giggled. "You're so full of it, Master Connor."

Rising, he took a long pull on the beer before saying, "That's my story and I'm sticking to it. Best remember that, girl, or I'll ask Master Grayson's permission to put you over my knee."

Heading for the stairs, Connor heard Caden say, "Damn, it's good to see him smiling again."

Shit, was I that bad? Climbing the stairs to the second-floor loft, he regretted worrying his only sibling and hoped his poor attitude continued to improve even though he still couldn't pinpoint the initial reason for it. He paused halfway up to enjoy the creative dance moves of two bare-breasted subs gyrating to the sultry voice of Rhianna as Greg and Devin stepped in with stern looks. Yanking them away from each other, the two Doms who were new members but long-time friends each delivered a resounding swat to their girl's ass before pressing them close to finish the dance. *Damn, I've really missed this place*, Connor mused, giving them a thumbs-up in approval as he continued upstairs.

They kept the lighting dimmer in the lofts, but he had no trouble making out each apparatus and the people enjoying them. Voices were more hushed but sharp cries of both pain and pleasure echoed from one end of the second level to the other. He spotted Grayson leaning against the back wall, hat tipped low, gaze intent on a sub bound facing their new A-frame and the man wielding a long, single leather strap standing behind her. Making his way toward the sheriff, Connor noticed a few new faces and knew he would have to catch up on the membership list soon.

"It appears to be a good addition." Connor nodded toward the frame, positioning himself next to Grayson.

"It's popular. Good to see you back. How's the shoulder?"

Grayson's gray-green eyes swiveled his way with concern.

Connor huffed a sigh at the standard greeting he was getting from everyone. "Sore and stiff. Relax, will you? I'm fine and yes, before you start nagging me like Caden, I'll be starting physical therapy on Monday. Hell, it can't be worse than what I've been through and I'm more than ready to pull my full weight around the ranch again."

Pushing away from the wall, Grayson reached out and squeezed his good shoulder. "Just don't overdo. I took a hit in the military while overseas, a through and through along my side. Hurt like a son-of-a-bitch, even more so when I pushed too hard too soon."

"I'll remember that. Go on. I'm sure Avery wants some attention. She looks like she's held up well from your trip back to Chicago. Finally nailed the bastards, huh?" Grayson's girl had shown admirable guts in getting evidence against two crooked cops who had plotted to set her up for the fall if their evidence thefts were discovered.

"They're going up for a long time," Grayson returned, his tone laced with the simmering anger he always exhibited when someone mentioned the threat to Avery's life that he'd helped her overcome. "And you're right, she needs some loving attention from her Master." A wicked gleam replaced the banked fury in his eyes.

"I've got this covered. Go have fun."

"I intend to. Later, Con."

Connor shook his head, wondering how both his brother and their friend and co-owner in the club had ended up tied down and happy about it within such a short time of each other. *Not me.* Nope, no way, no how. He was perfectly content playing the field, pausing to indulge in a monogamous relationship for a few months every so often, and when the novelty wore off, moving on without regrets. He'd made the mistake of allowing his relationship with Annie to go on too long, hadn't heeded the signs of her growing fonder of him than he was comfortable with or wanted. Her deflection had hurt, and pissed him off, but when he'd gotten over his ire, he'd known the blame lay on his shoulders, that it was him turning a blind eye to her feelings that had driven her to such extreme measures to get his attention.

Annie had followed her lover back to Bozeman without a word to Connor and he hoped she was happy. As for him, he was working his way back, both from the slump that had hit him with unexpected suddenness last fall and from the painful consequences of his ill-advised chase a few weeks ago. The only thing still sticking in his craw about that debacle was their failure to catch the rustlers, and he knew he wouldn't rest until the thieves were stopped. Ranchers around here were possessive of their livestock and their land; each head and every acre considered a valuable asset. They would get them, he didn't doubt that, but fuck, the waiting pissed him off.

Connor scanned the loft again, a slow, thorough sweep of each scene to ensure nothing was amiss. It was rare for a member to break a rule, but everyone here was only human, and mistakes were inevitable. He could remember a time, not so long ago, when he had enjoyed watching others so much the voyeurism had left him primed and ready to indulge himself by the time his duty as monitor ended. But as the hour dragged on, and he made several slow walk-throughs of the loft that circled around to encompass both sides of the lower space, he couldn't seem to drum up much enthusiasm to pick a play partner to end the evening with.

Frustrated with his continued lack of willingness to indulge himself despite his upbeat mood, he thought about slipping out and heading home as he spotted Dan climbing the stairs to relieve him as monitor. And then his gaze landed on a spanking bench where Master Brett now had Sue Ellen strapped face-down. Without pausing a beat in caressing his wife's reddened, tormented ass with one hand while thrusting between her spread legs with the other, Brett whipped his head around, caught Connor's look and beckoned him over.

The devoted married couple often invited a third to join them, and the thought of a ménage stirred Connor's interest in a way that had been lacking for far too long. With a welcome surge of anticipation and small sigh of relief, he nodded to Dan, who waved him on.

"Good to see you here, Master Connor," Brett greeted Connor as he reached them.

"It's good to be feeling up to coming back," he returned, meaning it. His blasé mental state might still linger but for the first time in weeks, his body roused in pleasure at the delectable feast before him. With her cheeks clenching, her pussy dripping and her dangling breasts tipped with tight, turgid nipples, Sue Ellen's body appeared ripe for fucking. "Has your lovely wife been acting up again?"

"Always." Brett's sigh indicated disappointment but the twinkle in his eyes as he tapped one puffy buttock belied his displeasure with his wife's attitude. "But she's taken her punishment like a good girl, so now she's earned a reward." Pulling his fingers from her swollen pussy, he bent over and asked her loud enough for Connor to hear, "You would enjoy sucking Master Connor's cock, wouldn't you, love?"

"Oh, yes, Master," Sue Ellen breathed, her excitement evident in her whispered reply.

Connor didn't need more of a verbal invitation than that and strode to the head of the bench as Brett shifted between her splayed knees. Both men released their cocks, sheathing themselves as Brett continued to fondle Sue Ellen's ass and Connor brushed his fingers over her trembling lips as she lifted her face. Her tongue darted out, licking the calloused pads of his fingers, the gesture sending a streak of heat up his arm. Pinching her chin, she opened for him, those lush lips wrapping around his girth like a warm glove as he pushed past them. He much preferred going bareback for oral, but respected Brett's insistence on a condom from anyone invited to pleasure his wife. Lucky for him, Sue Ellen was so talented at fellatio he could feel every stroke of her tongue, every nip along his shaft and each hard suck through the thin latex.

Grasping her head, he tunneled his fingers into her hair and held tight to her scalp as Brett surged into her from behind. Her low moan vibrated around his cock, the sensation drawing his own groan. Pulling back, he returned with a throat-bumping surge that she accepted by swirling her tongue in a teasing glide under his crown. He shook from the caress against that sensitive area, her mouth tightening as she took him deep again.

Whether it was the long abstinence or Brett's sudden, increasing strokes that were powerful enough to creak the apparatus and shift Sue Ellen's bound body that was responsible for the quick release of sperm from his balls, Connor didn't know. But as Sue Ellen worked him over good and pleasure ripped up his jerking cock, spewing into the condom, he really didn't care what the reason for his lack of control was.

"*Fuck*," he swore, ripples of heat spreading through his long-deprived body, his senses wallowing in the pleasure even as he was withdrawing from her hot mouth. The sudden need to walk away, end this before he was forced to say something nice in appreciation, clawed at him. Drawing on his years as a considerate Dom, he refrained from giving in to that urge as he disposed of the condom in a corner bin and returned to the couple that had been so generous with him.

Sue Ellen fell against her husband as soon as he released her and helped her off the bench. Connor's chest tightened at the look on Brett's face as he stroked her trembling, glistening body. *Did everyone have to be so blissfully content with their significant others lately*? Why that should bother him, he had no answer for. Reaching out, he stroked the back of Sue Ellen's head and bent to kiss her cheek.

"Thank you, sweetie. It was a pleasure." With a nod to Brett, he pivoted and returned downstairs, opting for a much-needed drink before heading home.

Nan, a leggy brunette with pretty, gold eyes smiled at him as he took a seat next to her at the bar. "Hello, Master Connor. You look good," she purred. Known and appreciated for her penchant for rough sex and an occasional bout of pain play, she'd been a favorite in the club for years and was well liked by both Doms and subs.

"Thank you, Nan, and right back at you." He appreciated her love of lingerie, like the siren red teddy hugging the fullness of her breasts with the lace-trimmed cutouts provided for protruding nipples. "Caden, get me my second beer, would you?"

"That was fast," his brother commented, handing over the cold bottle. "Couldn't find anyone to linger with upstairs?"

Connor turned away from his shrewd gaze and caught the gleam of interest reflected on Nan's face. She was a preference of his, both to hook up with for a few hours and as a friend and experienced sub he could trust not to develop an emotional attachment, but again, the interest to go there seemed to elude him.

"On the contrary," he answered. "Brett was in the mood to indulge Sue Ellen."

Before either Caden or Nan could comment, Sydney sidled up to the bar, smiling at Nan. "There you are. You're late tonight."

"I got tied up chatting before closing the tea shop." Nan looked at Caden and Connor, adding, "Tamara Barton has returned to town and we were catching up."

An unexpected jolt went through Connor at hearing Tam's name again. Other than the few words she allowed him at her father's funeral last year, he hadn't seen much of the heir of the neighboring ranch in the last five years, having only caught a glimpse of her from afar the times she'd returned for a visit. He still harbored a fringe of guilt from their last encounter. Frowning, he asked Nan, "Last I heard, she was getting married. Are the two of them planning on settling at the Barton ranch?" An uncomfortable tightness filled his chest at the thought.

Nan shrugged. "She refused to say anything about her engagement or fiancé, only that she planned to stay for now. She mentioned needing to address some personal issues and see to the ranch."

"You mean there's someone in Willow Springs I haven't met yet?" Sydney wanted to know.

"I'll introduce you when she has time," Nan offered. "I've known Tamara since grade school. We were close even though she was a year behind me. You and Avery will like her."

Connor didn't doubt that. The girl he remembered, despite the regrettable circumstances of the last time they'd spoken, was a sweet-natured dare-devil he used to enjoy watching from across the fields as she rode her powerful, sleek Arabian stallion with fearless abandon. Tam had just finished earning a master's degree and had returned home for a visit before taking a job in Boise when they'd last spoken. He still winced whenever the image of her pale, stricken face popped into his head unbidden, the hurt in her smoky eyes cutting him to the quick. Telling himself her impetuousness had left him with no choice but to go off on her hadn't eased his conscience then and still didn't now.

"Her foreman's been running the ranch since her father's death and seems to be doing a good job. Jason was the one who got a close enough look he could pass on a vague description of one of our rustlers after he spotted them hightailing it off his land a few weeks ago. He was smart enough not to go chasing after them," Caden reminded Connor.

"Yeah, yeah." Sliding off the stool, he tipped his hat. "I think I've heard enough about that. I'm out of here."

"Drive safe," Sydney said, giving him a quick hug.

"Yes, Mom," he drawled, tugging on her hair before turning

his back on their chuckles. Good-natured teasing aside, he'd gown tired of the molly-coddling, concerned glances and lectures. The sooner he got his strength back and resumed his regular duties around the ranch, the better all around.

Connor returned to his sprawling ranch home situated five miles from Caden's house, an itchiness having settled between his shoulder blades he couldn't seem to scratch. He usually left the club satisfied and ready to turn in, but as he padded into his bedroom and stripped, he couldn't shove aside the mention of their neighbor's return and the regret hearing Tam's name always stirred up. He fell face first into bed wishing they could go back to being friends who shared a special bond instead of the angry, hurt adversaries they'd ended up as when she'd left town. He hadn't let himself think about their last encounter and the harsh words he'd spoken to her in a long time, but as he fell asleep, the memory of that morning slid past his guard to disturb his dreams again.

"Christ, sweetie, you're so fucking wet and hot as a firecracker," Connor panted, tightening his hands on Darby's hips as he pounded into her. It was rare for him to invite a sub from the club home with him, but something had driven him to issue an invitation to Darby after he'd finished a scene with her at The Barn. She was one of the members who only visited their private BDSM venue a few times a year, but when she did, she was primed and ready to indulge whoever was lucky enough to get her attention. Last night it had been him.

The rustle of the hay bale he had her bent over and their harsh breathing were the only sounds in his small stable. The early morning sun streaking through the open doors behind him splashed a swath of yellow light across their sweat-slick bodies. Her bound hands clenched into fists above her pink buttocks as he ground into her quivering pussy from behind, her small mewls of pleasure accompanying the spasms rippling along his cock.

"Sir, please… I need to come," she pled before burying small white teeth into her lower lip.

"Now, Darby." Connor damn near saw stars as she convulsed around

his pistoning shaft and soaked him with her climax. By the time the overhead beams came back into focus, he was pulling from her clutching grips. "Hold on, sweetie," he instructed the still panting woman who lay with her cheek pressed against the hay, her eyes closed as she shuddered with lingering pleasure.

He disposed of the condom in a trashcan, adjusted his jeans and helped her stand. When he had awoken that morning, he'd slipped out of bed, hoping she would just take off while he was feeding the horses, but she had both irritated and surprised him when she'd walked into the stable naked, the look on her face revealing her desire for one more fuck before she left. Unable to resist such a tempting package, he'd shoved aside the annoyance at her delayed departure and gave her what she wanted. He hated disappointing subs.

Removing the leather tie around her wrists, he turned her in his arms, noting the redness covering her breasts and belly from the way his powerful thrusts had pushed her torso back and forth on the scratchy straw. The sated look in her eyes and contented sigh as he traced a finger over the marred skin drew his slow smile and mellowed his initial pique from her lingering presence.

"Thank you, Master Connor." Reaching behind his head, she drew his mouth to hers and initiated a kiss of gratitude he finished with a hard possession of her lips and mouth.

"You're welcome." Swatting her ass, he ordered in a light tone, "Now scram. I have things to do."

Scampering toward the doors with a giggle and small finger wave, Darby stopped short and uttered a soft, "Oh," that sent Connor's gaze flying to the doorway.

Shock held him immobile and mute for several seconds as he stared in disbelief at young Tam, the neighbor girl he possessed a special fondness for, peeking around the corner, her eyes wide with disbelief and interest, her face glowing bright red from embarrassment. Fury unlike anything he'd experienced before spread through him like a tsunami, dousing what lingering pleasure he still felt from his and Darby's morning coupling.

"Uh, I'll just get going," Darby mumbled, sidling past Tam and dashing

up to the house as Connor ate up the distance between him and the wide-eyed intruder.

Grasping her arm, he demanded in a furious voice, still shaken by what she'd witnessed, "What the hell *do you think you're doing?"*

"I… I'm sorry. I… was just… I came by to see… Gee, Con, I guess the rumors are true…"

A hint of lust entered her eyes, a look that shook him and added to his unaccustomed anger. "You have no business dropping in on me, Tamara, and sure as hell shouldn't be spying on a private tryst. When are you going to grow up?" Needing to wipe away the physical longing etched on her face, he yanked her over to her tethered horse and all but tossed her up into the saddle. "Damn it, girl, go home and quit being a fucking nuisance! I have better things to do than to constantly deal with your adolescent antics."

Shock wiped away the desire he found so uncomfortable. She spun her horse around on a tortured sob, her tear-filled eyes and pale face cutting through his ire. "Ah, shit, what have I done?" Shaking his head at his uncharacteristic display of temper, he swore he'd track her down later and apologize, his off-the-charts reaction baffling him as much as he had hurt her.

CONNOR AWOKE, promising himself he'd look up Tam as soon as he got a chance. He'd been caught so unaware by her presence and the interest she'd shown, he hadn't thought straight and didn't mean what he'd said. She'd moved away within weeks of that incident, refusing to talk to him or see him before accepting a job in Boise, and had avoided all opportunities to be alone with him whenever she returned for a visit. He finally managed to corner her in front of others at Richard's funeral, but she'd only paused for a moment, long enough for him to convey his condolences before walking away, leaving their previous parting unresolved. Now she was back, maybe for good, and the yearning to resume their friendship that had plagued him all this time tugged even harder at him.

Chapter 2

Leaning her forearms on the fence rail, Tamara Barton gazed across the field, enjoying the whiff of fresh air, the sound of lowing cattle and the sight of her grayish-white stallion prancing alongside her newest purchase, a pretty, dappled mare. Damn, she had missed viewing this serene vista every day, the wide-open spaces of her land, the peaceful quietness of country living as opposed to the hustle and bustle and constant noise of city life. She'd tried, God knows how hard she had tried to make a go of it in Boise, but the call of home wouldn't release its hold on her and after careful contemplation, she decided to move back.

Her father's unexpected death last year had left her shaken and added a new excuse for her to continue floundering in indecision over her future, but also gave her one more reason to return home. She would have thought the way her mother had abandoned her to a father and stepmother she'd never met before taking off with her current flavor of the month when Tamara had been ten-years-old would have rendered her hard-hearted enough to withstand the grief of losing a second parent. But it hadn't, and she missed the gruff, much older man more than she could say. She never expected to lose him so soon. A smile kicked up the corners of her mouth as she recalled how happy both Richard and his wife, Amy had been to welcome her to the ranch.

And now it was hers, all ten thousand acres of Montana land with the picturesque view of snow-capped mountains surrounding fields and woods for as far as the eye could see. A pang clutched her chest as she thought of the cost of inheriting at the age of thirty. Tamara added not returning sooner at her father's request to the list of regrets she had amassed since leaving her beloved home five years ago. Her struggle to forge a new life for herself and put a certain cowboy out of her mind ensured she remained away from the neighboring ranch whenever she'd returned for a visit, but it had been difficult keeping her distance. She had limited herself to spending time on the Barton spread with her father and Amy and making the trip into Willow Springs to visit friends when she knew Connor Dunbar would be working, but the desire to venture over there, just for a glimpse of him had been a constant pull.

When she'd spotted his tall form at the cemetery last year, a curl of resentment took up residence in her abdomen despite the pleasure seeing him always wrought. She'd wanted to blame him for the time she'd lost with her dad by moving away, just as she tried blaming him because she'd finally caved to Jeremy's pursuit of her as soon as she returned to Boise after the funeral and for letting that relationship go further than was right considering her tepid feelings. But it wasn't Connor's fault his feelings didn't run as deep or in the same direction as hers for him.

Another grip tightened her chest, this one forcing her to push off the rail and bring her fingers to her lips to let out a shrill whistle. With head and tail high, her Arabian, Galahad came trotting over with a soft whinny of welcome.

"You're always glad to see me, aren't you, pretty boy?" she crooned to the stallion before grabbing his mane and swinging up onto his back. Powerful muscles bunched under her thighs as he pranced in excited anticipation. Leaning over his neck, she brought her mouth near his twitching ear. "You and me, Galahad, just like always. Go!" With a nudge to his heaving sides, he bolted across the meadow.

The ground thundered beneath them as Tamara basked in the sense of freedom and the thrill of chasing the wind. This was a pleasure she couldn't get living in the city, an escape that never failed to ease her worries and regrets. On the back of her beloved steed, she could forget the hurtful words hurled at her by the one person she couldn't seem to get out of her system no matter how hard she tried or how far she ran. She'd been pining for Connor since her first summer in Montana and her ten-year-old heart had rolled over at her first glimpse of his startling blue eyes, and nothing had changed in the two decades since.

He wasn't for her, he'd made that clear over the years, but she hadn't listened until he'd shocked her with his uncharacteristic anger and cruel words. She was older now, wiser and hopefully hardened against the impact he'd always had on her. At least, that's what she was counting on. Between her new job and the responsibilities of running the ranch, she would be busy enough that thoughts of her neighbor shouldn't intrude on her life anymore.

By the time Tamara steered Galahad back toward the stable where Lady, his new companion was waiting in the attached corral, her muscles were aching, her cheeks chafed from the wind and her hair draped down her back in a tangled mess. Sliding off his back, she leaned against his warm bulk, feeling much better than when she'd ventured out from the house in a melancholy mood. Confident she could face the sad memories waiting for her inside and keep other unwanted thoughts at bay, she groomed Galahad, tossed each horse a scoop of their favorite pellets and left the barn.

"Hey, Tamara, hold up a sec, would you?" Jason, her foreman called out.

Halting halfway across the lawn and drive, she pivoted and walked toward her father's right-hand man. A tall, lean man in his late fifties, he'd been hired by her dad several years before Richard's health had taken a turn for the worse last year. She didn't know Jason well, but from her scan of the books last night, the ranch appeared to be running smoothly and turning a profit, and she figured he had a lot to do with that.

"Isn't Sunday your day off?" she asked as he smiled at her. His green eyes stood out against a tanned, craggy face any woman would find attractive. As with most men she thought appealing, she couldn't seem to drum up anything more than a mild interest and appreciation for a friend. Besides, from what she'd noticed, he had eyes on her stepmother.

"It is, but I wanted to ride out to the north pasture to check on the new calves before taking off for Billings. I saw you coming in and thought I'd pass on that they look hale and hearty, should bring in high dollars in a few years. I noticed a few mature head ready to cut from the herd and sell but wanted to run that by you before I left so I can add them to the roster for later this week."

"My dad trusted you to know what's what, so I'll go with whatever you think. If you're good with continuing to run things as you have been, I'd appreciate it. I start work tomorrow and will be in Willow Springs at the clinic on Mondays, Wednesdays and Fridays, which won't leave me much time to stay on top of all the details of running the ranch." Tamara wished she could have made working the ranch a priority; that would have pleased her dad. But the desire to get her money's worth out of her master's degree and work a few more years in her chosen field took precedence. She hadn't expected to inherit the reins to the Barton spread so soon and figured it wasn't going anywhere, so she would have time to become more involved in the day-to-day decisions later. "Is the new hand working out any better?" She'd met their most recent employee a few days ago and was reserving judgment as his air of insolence and laziness hadn't left a very good first impression.

"You know I'm happy to stay on with you and am still undecided on Neil Anders. I'm hoping he's just having trouble getting acclimated around here and isn't as shiftless as he's coming across." He reached out and squeezed her shoulder. "Your dad was a good man, someone I respected and admired because he always gave people the benefit of the doubt. He's missed around here."

She nodded and spun around, blinking back tears. "Thanks, Jason." With a backward wave, she trotted up to the house, relieved Amy was off visiting her sister in Bozeman for the weekend and wouldn't return until late the next day. Although she adored her stepmother, Amy had been hovering since Tamara had returned and it was nice to have some breathing room and the day to herself to prepare for her new job. She intended to stay busy enough to keep one blue-eyed cowboy from intruding on her thoughts.

Stepping into the wide, tiled foyer of the rustic ranch home, nostalgia struck her again. Straight ahead, hanging above the stone fireplace, a picture of her father and Amy greeted anyone entering their house. At the age of forty-two, Richard had been a confirmed bachelor and had never tired of telling Tamara how he'd fallen head over heels in love with confirmed bachelorette Amy when they'd met at a New Year's Eve party. Married a scant three months later, he often relayed with a beaming smile how much Tamara's sudden, unexpected presence had disrupted their lives on their six-year anniversary in the most wonderful way, saying she was the best thing to come from his wild, single days.

She may have spent the first ten years of her life with a neglectful, self-centered mother, Tamara reflected, but the following nineteen years she'd had with her father had made up for it. With a sigh, she padded into the great room where Amy's renovation of taking down the wall separating it from the kitchen was still a messy work in progress. As soon as Tamara settled in, she hoped to have plans drawn up to start building her own place. As much as she loved her stepmother, she didn't want to live with her forever. Wading through the mess, she put together a sandwich and then spent the evening finishing her unpacking.

Mental and physical exhaustion pulled at her by the time she stowed her emptied suitcases in the walk-in closet of the room she had occupied since her first night on the ranch. As she slid into bed, her phone buzzed and she reluctantly checked the caller ID. *Damn, so close.* Guilt and exasperation rushed to the surface as she thought about ignoring her ex-fiancé's call, but she knew from experience that would just be putting it off. In the month since she'd called off their wedding, Jeremy had refused to accept they couldn't fix whatever had changed her mind.

"Jeremy," she sighed, answering the phone. "It's late."

"It's not even ten, baby."

She hated when he called her that generic nickname, and he knew it. "I have to get up early. There are chores I need to see to before going to work."

His heavy sigh came through the phone loud and clear. "I thought you had hired hands for that."

"That doesn't mean I shouldn't pull my weight and take care of my own horse myself."

"Look, I know you feel bad about your dad's passing, but that doesn't mean you have to bury yourself out in the boonies. I tried calling you earlier, but you didn't answer."

The slight admonishment in his tone grated on her nerves, as did his refusal to understand she *wanted* to be here, but she forced herself to remember she had wronged him by letting their relationship get as far as it did when she had known her heart wasn't in the right place to make such a commitment. "Sorry. I went riding and didn't take my phone." Which hadn't been by mistake.

"That was irresponsible," he chided. "See, there's another example of why you need me. What if you had fallen and gotten hurt?"

Tamara laughed. "I haven't toppled off a horse in ages. Besides, I've told you, this is a working ranch. There are hands around if someone finds themselves in need of help. I'm tired, Jeremy, and need to get up early."

"I just wanted to wish you luck tomorrow. Besides, we spent over a year not going to sleep without telling each other good night."

"But we're not a couple any longer," she reminded him as gently as she could while grinding her teeth together.

"We will be as soon as you get over whatever's bothering you. You need to tell me so we can at least begin hashing this out," he insisted for about the hundredth time since she'd broken off their engagement.

Tamara hated to do it but saw no other choice. She needed to get firm and end this once and for all, even if it meant hurting a good, decent man whose only fault was falling in love with a woman who couldn't love him back the way he deserved.

"Enough, Jeremy. I'm sorry, but I don't love you, maybe I never did. And that's not something you can change, or we can work out. Please, don't contact me again. Goodbye." She hung up with a heavy heart, sadness pulling her down as she crawled into bed. Jeremy had been nothing but good to her and knowing the pain of unrequited feelings made her feel that much worse over the way she had treated him.

She fell asleep remembering the afternoon she met her father's neighbor and how her tender young heart had fallen for a shining knight sitting astride a huge horse with the confidence born of experience and age rushing to her rescue. Little had she known then that one look into those cobalt eyes would seal her fate for years to come.

Tamara broke away from her new classmates to stand in line with much younger kids at the horse-riding ring, her heart beating faster with every step that brought her closer to her turn. She had only been living with the father she'd never met before for a few weeks after her mother had abandoned her in favor of taking off with her current boyfriend. Fear of being tossed aside again had been her constant companion, making her desperate to not only fit in at school, but to make Richard Barton and his wife proud enough to want to keep her. Admitting the couple had been nothing but kind and welcoming wasn't enough to ease her insecurity.

The county fair the school had bussed them to for a day of fun to end the school year with was a new experience for her and she'd been enjoying the games and rides and the way her friends didn't hesitate to include her. But when she spotted the horseback riding, she saw an opportunity she couldn't resist. Everyone on the ranch could ride horses and all of her new friends boasted about riding. Here was a chance to accomplish a feat sure to impress and please her father and give her something in common with the other kids.

Her determination didn't keep her from shaking as she watched the large animals trotting around the ring, the young riders bouncing on their backs. Her father had showed her around his ranch when she'd first arrived, warning her to stay clear of the horse's hooves. But there was so much more to scare her than those heavy hooves. Having never even owned a dog, she found herself both fascinated and frightened by the horse's beauty and size.

I can do this, *Tamara told herself as one of the teenagers helping out opened the gate for her to enter. Keeping her eyes glued to the silky brown coat covering the bunching muscles of the next horse being led up to mount, she struggled to swallow past her dry throat.*

"Are you ready, kid?" The tall girl bent and cupped her hands, waiting to boost her up, way up into the saddle. When Tamara hesitated, she cocked her head, asking, "What's wrong? Haven't you ridden before?" Disbelief underscored her words, as if it was unheard of to have reached the age of ten and finished the fifth grade in Willow Springs, Montana without knowing how to ride.

Squaring her small shoulders, Tamara ignored the blush stealing over her face, keeping her eyes averted from the much younger kids already mounted and laughing in enjoyment. Shoring up her resolve to fit in as fast as possible so she could stay, she kept quiet and put her foot in the older girl's hands. "Grab the pommel, kid," she snapped when Tamara gasped as she found herself hoisted up in the air and then leaning against the heaving side of the animal. She didn't know what a pommel was but latched onto a protrusion on the front of the creaking saddle and pulled herself up. "There you go. You're new around here, aren't you? Maybe I should walk you around for a bit first," the teen offered as Tamara swayed and squeezed her eyes shut.

Opening them again, she looked straight ahead instead of down and shook her head, determined to accomplish this feat on her own. "I… I'm good."

"Okay, if you're sure. Just follow the horse in front of you three times around."

With a white-knuckled grip on the reins, Tamara sucked in a deep breath as the horse fell in line behind the one in front of them. She scanned the park, amazed at how far she could see from her high perch. The slow pace soon lulled her into relaxing and becoming accustomed to the strange feel of the animal moving under her. After one loop, she forgot the mortification of being five years older than any other kid in the ring and got brave enough to reach a trembling hand out to touch the soft mane hanging down the horse's neck.

The sudden shift of its head and quick prance of its feet caught her off guard and with only one hand on the reins, she couldn't stop from sliding sideways. Before she could catch enough breath to cry out, a hard arm swooped around her waist and righted her in the saddle, a deep voice reaching past the roaring in her head.

"There you go, sweetie. You're okay." The owner of that soothing voice tightened his arm as she grasped the reins with both hands again.

With nausea churning in her quivering stomach, she looked over and up into a tanned face shadowed by a lowered cowboy hat. Tamara watched, mesmerized as the older boy nudged his hat back, revealing eyes the color of the cloudless sky. Her racing heart slowed and then went pitter patter until he removed his arm.

With a nod and small curl of his lips, he nudged both horses into a slow walk, staying alongside her as he said, "Deep breath. You'll get the hang of it. Move your body with the horse, yes, like that. These fillies are sweet and mellow, just the right temperament for newbie riders. Are you visiting someone in the area?"

Was it any wonder she remained overly conscious of her status as the new kid? Everyone seemed to know everyone else in this small town, something she wasn't familiar with having grown up with a mother who moved from one big city to another every year or two. She shook her head, her hackles up as she replied in a defensive tone, "No, I live on the Barton Ranch."

His small grin spread to a smile and her heart executed a funny roll. "You're old man Barton's daughter. I'm Connor Dunbar. We're neighbors. Once you get your bearings, you can ride over to our place for a visit, and from the looks of you now, that won't take long. What's your name?"

"Tamara."

"Well, Tam, you've got a good seat, you just need confidence and practice."

Pleased, liking the way he shortened her name, she realized they'd finished the second loop without her panicking again. Something about the way Connor looked at her, as if she was special, warmed her where she'd been so cold since her mother's desertion. Not that her father had been unkind, just the opposite in fact. Both he and Amy seemed pleased to have her around. But she'd grown up knowing nothing was permanent, which had kept her from believing this time would be different.

"Thank you," she said as another older teen called to him.

With a wave, he turned his horse with an expertise she envied, flashing another devastating smile that disrupted her young heart. "Catch you later, neighbor."

Tamara watched him trot off, vowing to master riding as fast as possible because now she had two people she yearned to make proud of her.

TAMARA AWOKE DISGRUNTLED at having her sleep disturbed by a reoccurrence of that memory, one she should have gotten over long ago. She'd been so young and scared when she had first come to Willow Springs, not to mention impressionable. That hadn't been the only time Connor had come to her rescue, and she had been unprepared for the impact his chivalry would leave on her broken, tender heart.

With a sigh, she rolled out of bed and dressed for her first day at the clinic. With any luck, the two doctors who ran the only medical facility in town would have a slew of patients in need of physical therapy to take her mind off a certain cowboy she'd tried and failed to forget during her time away. She made the twenty-minute drive into Willow Springs with tired, gritty eyes and a determination to move forward with her life without looking back. If she'd learned one thing from her relationship with Jeremy, it was not to settle. She had returned home to find the happiness that had eluded her in the years away, and if that meant waiting, taking her time to search not only for what she needed to attain that goal, but to get it from the right person, then so be it.

She hit the city limits and waved to a few early morning pedestrians as she drove past the small hubbub of the town square on her way to the clinic. Nothing much had changed since she'd left town. The hangouts where she'd spent so much time as a teenager were still as popular now, and other than a few new businesses, Willow Springs hadn't grown much. She wished she had put out more effort to see her friends during her many return trips home. Other than to visit with Nan at her teashop and go into Billings with her for a day of shopping and lunch, she hadn't visited other friends and acquaintances she'd known for years. Nan had laid into her the other day when Tamara stopped by her teashop for the first time since moving back. After her usual lecture for going away in the first place, she'd brought tears to Tamara's eyes with a crushing hug and heartfelt, "Damn, I'm glad you're back for good" whisper.

Connor Dunbar's painful rebuke the day she'd ridden to his place to talk to him about the job offer in Boise and instead ended up spying on him and some girl going at it in his barn had sent her running so fast, Tamara hadn't stopped long enough to tell anyone except her father and Amy she'd decided to take the job. The only thing that had kept her from accepting it had been the thought of moving away from Connor, but after he'd laid into her and made his feelings crystal clear, she no longer had that excuse to stay around here. She had been so hurt, jealous and confused by her reaction when she'd stumbled upon that unexpected scene, she'd kept everything about that encounter to herself. Even though she suspected Amy might have an inkling her taking off that way had something to do with Tamara's unrequited infatuation with Connor, neither of them had brought it up yet.

As Tamara parked and strolled into the back entrance of the clinic where the physical therapy room was located, she tried shoving aside intruding memories best left in the past, but when had she ever succeeded with putting her feelings for Connor on the back burner? She'd applied for the new physical therapist position online, interviewed for it over the phone and accepted the job via e-mail. Other than visiting with Nan at her tea shop on Friday, today was the first day since moving back two weeks ago that she would get reacquainted with a few more people. That prospect lightened her step.

The morning staff meeting went longer than she planned for and after thanking everyone for their warm welcome she dashed back down the hall to the physical therapy room. Furnished with two raised mats, a set of parallel bars, pulleys along one wall to go along with the various exercise equipment hanging up and a small desk in the far corner, it appeared to have everything she needed. The space wasn't big or fancy, but it was all hers and would work well. Padding over to her desk, she planned to check the scheduled appointments for the day but the bell above the door pealed as someone entered, diverting her attention.

Tamara pivoted, her eyes widening as none other than the object of her obsession for the last twenty years entered with a loose-limbed stride that never failed to draw women's attention, including her own. Connor Dunbar looked the same at thirty-eight as he had five years ago; ruggedly handsome with sun-streaked, dark brown hair worn long enough to pull back in a short ponytail, his jaw covered with scruffy whiskers a shade darker than his hair that was sexy as hell.

"Tam?" Surprise colored his voice as those incredible eyes landed on her frozen stance.

The slow stretch of his chiseled lips hit her with a gut-wrenching sucker punch as warmth encircled her heart. *No, no, no*, she lamented, resisting the urge to turn and bang her head against the wall. That reaction would not do. She'd stayed away so long to get over him, praying with endless regularity for a much less potent response when seeing him again. Disappointment swamped her upon learning those pleas had gone unanswered. Given she'd returned to put this ridiculous, one-sided infatuation to bed once and for all, her response didn't bode well for achieving that goal anytime soon. *I can do this, remain professional and do my job,* she lectured herself. *Easy. Piece of cake.* And then a blue flame of pleasure lit up his eyes as he strode toward her, shredding her resolve in less time than it took to come up with it.

"I heard you were back, maybe for good." Gripping her shoulders with his large, calloused hands, he pulled her close for a bear hug she knew meant nothing more than an old friend greeting another. "It's damn good to see you, sweetie."

Tamara stiffened, the endearment a reminder he would never consider her anything more than a friend. Pulling back from the comfort of his muscled body, she cast a quick glance down at the list of appointments and saw what she hadn't had time to check. He was her first patient. Dismay changed to sudden concern, overruling her silent objection as the meaning of that sunk in.

"What happened? Were you injured?"

Connor looked puzzled and then his face cleared with a rueful twist of his lips. Rotating his left shoulder, he nodded to the computer. "It's in my file, I'm sure. Gunshot wound several weeks back, followed by surgery to repair some damaged tendons. I believe it's your job to help me gain as much strength back as possible."

Shot? Tamara pulled back from the urge to sink onto the desk chair before her wobbly legs took the choice from her. Instead, locking her knees, she reminded herself of her job. Given her reaction to seeing him again was as strong as always, she wasn't happy about having to put her hands on him or with being subjected to his close presence for a few weeks. *It is what it is, so get over it already*. She'd been repeating that phrase for a long time and it looked like she would continue to do so.

Chapter 3

She hasn't changed. The relief Connor experienced at that thought went along with the familiar rush gazing at Tamara Barton always gave him. He'd never been able to pinpoint what it was about the neighbor kid that made him want to smile and pulled on his protective instincts every time he saw her. He'd found himself drawn to the determination tightening her small, pale face the first time he'd laid eyes on her at the county fair. That same tug had yanked at him when he'd seen her pale, tear ravaged face at her father's funeral last year, leaving him frustrated when she'd turned away from him after his brief condolences. Now, the surprised pleasure that had shone in her gray eyes before switching to concern put him in a much better mood than when he'd arrived at the clinic cursing the necessity for therapy to his injured rotator cuff.

"You can fill me in after I look at your chart," she said now, the worry and censure in her tone tickling him.

"I can, can I?" he drawled. "You always did fret like a mother hen." For some reason that didn't bug him as much as when his well-meaning friends and soon-to-be sister-in-law did the same thing.

"Because you've always been reckless to the point of careless. Oh." Tam's eyes clouded as she scanned through his chart. Shaking her head, she sent him a familiar rueful glance that tightened his abdomen. "Chasing after rustlers by yourself? You're lucky you didn't end up with a lot worse."

He knew that and was tired of the reminders. "I wasn't about to just let them drive off. You should be more thankful. I believe they've hit your ranch, as well as ours and a few others."

"I could never be grateful for you putting yourself in harm's way, Connor."

And there it was, that light in her eyes as she gazed at him that set off alarm bells. What was it about that soft look that both stirred Connor and made him itch to run away? He'd had countless women look at him with lust and a handful with a hint of stronger feelings than he cared for, including Annie. Some of them he had enjoyed before sending them on their way. The others he'd let down as gently as possible before breaking it off or refused to let things get to the intimate stage. With Tam, he'd done neither and never could come up with a reason why.

Removing his Stetson, he shrugged off her concern and set it on the desk. "It wasn't a big deal. A little residual weakness is all that's left of the encounter, which is why I'm here, putting myself at your mercy," he teased.

"You are never at anyone's mercy," she countered with the ease of someone who knew him well. "Sit on the mat and let me check your range of motion to start. How much pain are you in?"

Connor sat on the raised, padded mat, dreading Tamara's hands on him. It wasn't the pain that worried him, but damned if he could understand what it was he was growing more and more uncomfortable with since walking in and discovering she would be his therapist despite being overjoyed at seeing and talking to her again. Like the rest of her, her hands were fine-boned and delicate, but when she placed them on his shoulder and lower arm and lifted, it didn't surprise him to feel the strength in her grip regardless of her slender frame. She'd grown into a talented, accomplished horsewoman since the day he rescued her from toppling off her first horse, and she'd been handling that massive steed of hers with admirable skill and strong arms since her father had gifted her with the colt on her sixteenth birthday.

What did surprise him and caught him off guard was the warmth spreading up his arm that had nothing to do with the pain radiating from his shoulder as she maneuvered the joint back and forth, up and down and then in circles. Shifting on the mat in uncomfortable awareness, he reminded himself of who she was. *This is Tam, the cute kid I've been looking out for for years. The young woman with stars in her eyes who has home and hearth written all over her*. He needed to remember that, repeat it as often as necessary to keep from putting a wedge in their special relationship again like he had before she moved away.

"Hurt?" she asked, raising his arm straight up.

"A little. Not bad."

She smirked, her pewter eyes twinkling as she looked down at him. "Would you admit it if it did?"

He grinned up at her and shook his head. "Nope."

"Men," she muttered, letting go of his arm. "You're stiff, the muscles are tight and weak. Knowing you, you probably ignored the doctor's orders to take it easy and not overdo."

She pivoted and walked over to a file cabinet next to the desk. Connor tried and failed not to notice the way her firm ass shifted under the loose uniform pants. Looking away, he gritted his teeth, chastising himself for wondering how those cheeks would look draped over his lap. Damn it, she wasn't for him, or anyone else to dally with for that matter. Her innocence had always appealed to him in an over-protective, macho manner and kept him from looking at her as anyone other than the young kid he'd befriended, and now the woman whose friendship he cherished and wanted back to keep. Not to mention whose well being he'd taken upon himself to ensure the first time he glimpsed the sheer grit etched on her pixie face as fear lurked in her eyes as she struggled to stay astride her first horse.

Connor stood as Tam walked back toward him holding several sheets of paper. "I'll go over some of these exercises and stretches with you and you can use the pulleys on the wall before you go. I recommend using the least amount of weight for now and to concentrate more on stretching and loosening the muscles than strengthening."

He looked at the sketches and frowned at the limitation she suggested. "I have a ranch to work. I can't remain in limbo much longer," he told her, trying to rein in his frustration. Inactivity didn't sit well with him.

"I know that, Con, but if you continue to do too much too soon, you'll only hinder your progress and extend the time it'll take to regain your full strength."

"Fine, show me these exercises and I'll give them a whirl."

"Hey," she tossed out, leading him over to the pulleys. "It's not my fault you were reckless enough to chase after rustlers by yourself. I wasn't even here when you behaved so foolishly."

At the reminder, Connor reached out and took her arm, turning her to face him. "About that morning at my place, Tam, you've never let me apologize in person and…" Before he could finish, she pulled from his light clasp and stepped back, her eyes cutting to his in a quick glance filled with chagrin and then sliding away again.

"Water under the bridge, Con. You don't need to say anything. I accepted your texted apology, several of them, if you'll recall. Now, why don't you try a few stretching maneuvers using this pulley? Concentrate on moving straight up and then all the way down. If it becomes too uncomfortable, stop. I need to check the rest of my schedule for today."

Instead of following her instructions, he took hold of her

stubborn chin and turned her to face him again. Tilting his head, he asked, "I didn't like it and I get why you avoided seeing me after I blew up at you, but why wouldn't you talk to me after your father's funeral?"

She sucked in a deep breath, her lips tightening before she replied, "I was a mess, Con, devastated, grief-stricken and not thinking straight. I'm sorry if I hurt you."

He didn't want to dredge up painful memories for her and drew on a fonder memory to lighten the sudden tension between them. Releasing her soft chin, he drawled, "That wasn't the first time I saw you when you were a crying mess. I helped then."

"Yes, well I'm not a seventeen-year-old whose prom date turned out to be a groping jerk," she countered with a small smile. It was her turn to cock her head as she asked, "Did I ever mention when I saw Billy Wilcox at school a few days later he'd been sporting a black eye?"

"You don't say. Let's hope he learned his lesson and kept from walking into any more doors. Let's do this." He nodded to the pulleys.

CONNOR'S MENTION of that day at his barn and then when they'd seen each other last year shook Tamara; she hadn't expected him to bring those days up, didn't want him to resurrect either painful episode. She'd been having enough trouble remaining both friendly and professional due to the shock of his unexpected presence. Their reunion had been inevitable, she'd known that, but even so, she still wasn't prepared for the impact of that searing blue gaze warming at the sight of her or her body's quick response to his nearness, to the feel of his strength under her hands.

Keeping one eye on his efforts at the pulley, she scanned the schedule, relieved to see the busy day ahead. With luck, concentrating on her new patients would keep her mind occupied enough to put off fretting over how she would ever get on with her life if she couldn't get past this infatuation without relinquishing a friendship she cherished. The hardest part about being away these past few years had been refusing to see Connor. At the time, she'd thought severing all communication with him had been the key to letting go of her hopes for a different kind of relationship with the man she shared a special bond with. Time, distance and allowing another man into her life had proved her wrong and it was disappointing to learn how poorly that sacrifice had failed. Her father's unexpected death was just one regret that showed her here was where she needed to be, where she now knew she wanted to stay.

Despite his weakened condition, Connor's deltoid and triceps brachii muscles still bulged under his light blue denim shirt as he worked through the stretching exercises. The muscled bulk he had amassed working the ranch would aid in his recovery, and she didn't doubt he would be up to par in no time and wouldn't require too many appointments with her.

A light sheen of perspiration spread over his tanned face as he grimaced with the last three repetitions. Shaking her head at his bullheadedness, she returned to his side and put her hand on his arm, halting the stretch in motion.

"I said to stop if it became too uncomfortable. You will do more damage than good if you push too hard."

"I'm fine," he returned with a touch of irritation.

Pushing to his feet, Connor's towering, broad-shouldered height of six-foot-three dwarfed her smaller, ten-inch shorter frame and sent a rush of familiar heat through her. His nearness had always given her a sense of comfort and safety, but it hadn't been until the summer she turned twenty that she experienced a pleasurable warmth from his closeness and the tenderness in his gaze to go along with those feelings for the first time. It was disconcerting to learn running away hadn't shaken them and time proved to be as ineffective.

Stepping back, Tamara returned to her desk and flipped through the schedule book. "We can do a follow-up next Monday morning, same time, if that works for you." That would give her a week to come to terms with her continued desire for a man who refused to regard her as anything more than the neighbor girl he was fond of.

"I can do that." Picking up his Stetson off the desk, he put it on and leveled his intent, probing gaze from under the lowered brim on her long enough to make her uncomfortable.

"What?" she snapped when he said nothing else.

Shaking his head, a rueful smile tugged at the corners of his mouth. "I was wondering where the years went. Wasn't it just yesterday you were a scared, gangly kid sliding off your first horse?"

"No, it wasn't. Twenty years have passed, Con, and I'm no longer a kid, haven't been for years now," she reminded him, for what little good it would do.

"But you're still young, and refreshingly innocent. I like that about you, sweetie."

Narrowing her eyes, she bit off, "Don't call me that." At his puzzled frown, she added, "It's not professional."

Another slow smile swept across his face and tightened the knot in her stomach. "Since when are we on a professional basis? Besides," he pivoted, tossing over his shoulder as he strode toward the door, "that's what I call all the girls."

"I know." Tamara assumed her whispery sigh fell on deaf ears as he walked out with a wave the same cocky grin and twinkle in his blue eyes that had turned her adolescent crush into a raging hormonal lust-fest the first time he aimed it her way and she'd been old enough to know what the clutch between her legs meant. That was her Connor, careless and carefree, and happy to stay that way. She'd grown up but doubted he ever would, or even wanted to.

Tamara did her best to put him out of her mind as she spent the rest of the day getting to know her patients and the staff at Willow Springs medical facility. She couldn't count how many times her over-protective father had rushed her to an emergency care clinic in Billings long before their small town boasted their own. Once she'd grown comfortable in the saddle and had fallen in love with the entire equine species, there had been no keeping her off horses. Her daredevil stunts earned her reprimands and hugs from her dad, rueful shakes of her stepmother's head and a few lectures from Connor as he gave her lessons on how to master the feat that sent her toppling off.

The first ten years of her life were marred by sadness and loneliness because of her mother's neglect, but the second decade made up for it. She had entered her twenties with a thrilling bang, falling head over heels in love and lust with her friend and oftentimes rescuer. But the last few years had been fraught with devastating pain and heartbreak that had begun with the rift between her and Connor and had escalated last year with her father's death.

While she drove home that afternoon happy about reconnecting with Connor again, the resurrection of her strong feelings reinforced her determination to find a way to get him out of her system once and for all. If she could just figure out how to do that.

AFTER COMPLETING a few errands around town, Connor entered Dales Diner at noon. One whiff of Ed and Clyde's cooking emanating from behind the long counter improved his already upbeat mood. Even though the workout Tam had put him through left his shoulder throbbing more than usual, he was so pleased the two of them had reconnected and agreed to put that last harmful incident behind them it was easy to ignore the aching soreness that irritated him. After hearing about her return, he'd guessed she was the new physical therapist and refrained from hightailing it over to the Dunbar ranch yesterday to put their relationship back together. He figured she wouldn't be able to avoid him at the clinic as easily as at home.

Damn, I've missed her. He hadn't realized how much until he'd set eyes on her pixie face again. He wondered if she had kept up with her riding skills while living in the city, and why she had cut her hair. The thick mass of inky, braided silk still hung down between her shoulders, but no longer reached her lower back.

As he wound his way through the tables to the back booth where Caden and Grayson already waited, he found himself hoping nothing else had changed about the girl he'd always been so fond of.

"Hey," he greeted his brother and the sheriff as he took a seat. "Did you order yet?"

"No, Avery's getting our drinks. She's bringing you a coke," Grayson replied.

"Your girl knows me too well. I have to say, I'm surprised she's still working here after landing the IT job in Billings." Avery's skills on the computer had aided her in finding evidence against two corrupt cops and had also endeared her to everyone in Willow Springs who benefitted from her expertise.

Grayson's eyes followed Avery as she made her rounds. "She didn't want to leave Gertie short-handed, and since she only has to make the trip to the Billings office twice a week and can work from my place the rest of the time, she wanted to help out here when needed."

"Order up, Gertie!" Clyde's voice rang out.

"Hold your friggin' horses. I've only got two hands," Gertie snapped, unconcerned with who heard her.

All three men smiled at the cantankerous owner's raspy voice.

Loyal to a fault, the widow still ran the popular eatery with a gruff disregard for polite manners. "At least Avery has quit stuttering around Gertie," Caden said as Grayson's girl returned with their drinks and smiled at him.

"I've learned her bark is much worse than her bite. Hi, Connor."

"Hey, sweetie." Connor paused, remembering Tam's comment she didn't think he heard. "Tell me something. Does it bother you when I call you sweetie?"

She shook her head. "No, why would it?"

He nodded, shoving aside the hurt reflected in Tam's eyes that popped into his head. "Exactly. I'll take the BLT and a double order of fries."

"So, did you keep your physical therapy appointment this morning?" Caden wanted to know after Avery had taken their orders. Reaching for his iced tea, his brother's look told Connor he expected his answer to be no.

"As a matter of fact, I did, and you'll never guess who the new therapist is."

Grayson frowned in thought. "There's no one new in town I know of."

"Tamara Barton's not a new resident," he said.

A smile creased Caden's weathered face. "That explains your good mood even though you want physical therapy like you want a hole in the head."

"Of course I'm happy she's back and was glad to see her again," he shot back, his tone defensive against the glint in his brother's identical blue eyes. "We've been neighbors for years."

"And your pissy mood when she left lasted for months," Caden reminded him.

Connor didn't debate him about that. He'd been both upset and ticked off from the way Tam had left town without even a goodbye and over the way she'd ignored his calls for weeks. She'd accepted his numerous apologies by text, ignored his pleas to get together and then let him know she'd accepted the job in Boise and was on her way to Idaho before he could say goodbye. If it hadn't been for her father's willingness to answer his inquiries about her whenever Connor happened to see Richard, he might have tracked her down and insisted she talk to him. The blame lay solely on his shoulders for her silence, forcing him to respect her wish for distance. He shouldn't have come down on her the way he had when he'd discovered she'd watched that entire scene in his barn. To this day, he didn't know if it was the shock of knowing the kid he'd befriended all those years ago had witnessed such a thing, or the way his sated cock had stirred again from the lust in her eyes that made him lash out at her and say things he never meant.

"Richard's death devastated her. I know she made frequent visits to the ranch, but I'm surprised she didn't move back before now." Grayson removed the toothpick nestled in the corner of his mouth as Avery returned with their order. Reaching for his plate, he drawled, "Thank you, sugar."

Caden picked up his burger, saying, "It surprised me she left at all. I wonder why she did."

"Who?" Avery asked him but it was Connor who answered.

"Tamara Barton, who inherited the ranch abutting ours last year after her dad died. Nice girl." He drilled Caden with a challenging glare his irritating brother ignored.

"Yeah, Nan mentioned she might join us tomorrow at her tea shop. I'm looking forward to meeting her. I'm clocking out, so I'll catch you later."

Grayson watched her stroll away, his eyes soft as he bit into his hoagie. Connor shook his head with a frown of mock disgust. "Whipped, both of you. It's nauseating."

Caden laughed and slapped him on the back hard enough to have him choking on a fry and reaching for his coke. "Someday, I'll enjoy watching you eat those words."

"Not me, no way, no how. Why settle for one entrée when I can indulge in a buffet any time I want?"

"Sometimes," Grayson said, his gray-green gaze shifting to watch Avery walking out, "you discover a new entrée that kills your taste buds for everything else."

Connor grunted, a taunting smile curving his lips. "Sap."

TIRES SCREECHING *to a halt broke through Tamara's misery and she lifted her tear-streaked face from her arms, somehow not surprised to see Connor hopping out of his truck and striding toward her. He'd been riding to her rescue now for seven years, and each time her heart thudded a little faster when those blue, blue eyes zeroed in on her with a look of exasperated fondness and overrated concern. She tried smiling up at him from her perch on the high school's front steps, but her mouth wobbled instead.*

"Hi," she sniffed,

As he squatted down in front of her, she couldn't help noticing the bulge of his thighs and the glint in his eyes as he caught her distressed appearance in the dim lighting. "What's up, sweetie?"

"Boys," she muttered.

"Be a little more specific, please."

She tightened her hand on her bodice, heat enveloping her face. "Billy Wilcox is a jerk."

His jaw went rigid but his hand was gentle as he cupped her chin, checked her face and then slid his eyes down to the popped buttons on the top of her green satin prom dress. "Are you okay?"

"Yes," she sighed, refusing to lie. "He just made me mad when he wouldn't stop kissing me after I said enough. This," she looked down at her top, "wasn't on purpose. I pulled away from him..."

"That's enough. Come on, I'll drive you home."

"Okay." Feeling better already, she pushed to her feet and leaned against his tall frame, a strange shiver rippling through her. He boosted her up into

his truck and leaned over her to fasten the seatbelt himself, his breath warm on her neck.

A longing swept through Tamara as he settled behind the wheel and wrapped one arm around her shoulders to pull her close as he drove. Her body felt strange, hot and cold all at once…

Tamara groaned and rolled over, shifting uncomfortably as she struggled to get back to sleep without plaguing memories haunting her. She drifted off again, this time her mind shifting to a later time and different scene, tiredness pulling her back under and leaving her powerless to stop the replay.

Her nipples beaded into tight pinpoints just from listening to Connor's commanding voice, her pussy went damp from eyeing his taut buttocks clenching as he drove into the woman bent over the stack of hay bales. Sweat popped out along her brow and her legs grew cramped from her crouched position behind the door to the barn. The woman's low moans switched to high-pitched wails as they climaxed together, the sight enough to make her fingers itch to slip inside her pants to tease her own orgasm to the surface as she eyed the bound, clenched hands of his willing partner. Bondage. *So, the rumors were true. She was still assimilating that fact and picturing herself in the woman's position as he helped her stand and Tamara noticed the bare flesh of her labia sported the same pinkness covering the woman's buttocks.*

Tamara grew hotter and her vaginal muscles spasmed as she imagined the pain of being slapped on such sensitive flesh. A sound escaped her tight throat, alerting the couple to her presence. Uh, oh…

Tamara awoke the next morning in a sweaty tangle of sheets, her body still shuddering from dreams that refused to leave her be, no matter how much time elapsed between the memories or how far she distanced herself from the man. Giving up on finding answers, she tumbled out of bed and padded into her attached bathroom. Amy ended up staying with her sister an extra day and planned to return today. It wouldn't do to let her stepmother see her in such a befuddled state. Amy knew of her infatuation and wouldn't need another reason to bring it up.

She felt better after lingering under a hot shower and

downing two cups of coffee. Unable to put it off any longer, she entered her father's office and took a seat behind his desk. Blinking back tears, she pulled up the ranch books and spent the morning going over the ledgers, noting the losses where rustlers had made off with a few head of cattle and the gains from the last sales. Profits remained marginal, but with any luck, Galahad's offspring would bring in some extra cash by this time next year.

The Dunbar Ranch was almost four times the size of hers and from what she'd read, they had suffered a significantly higher number of losses from the thieves, so she counted herself, Amy and their few employees lucky in that aspect. It was no wonder Connor's frustration pushed him into going off half-cocked after them.

Spending time with him again had reinforced how much she'd missed him, her reaction to one look from his searing blue eyes confirming she'd made the right decision in calling off her engagement. She was fond of Jeremy, but she couldn't marry one man when she was in love with another. Her tepid responses to him during sex should have alerted her much sooner that it would never work, and she accepted full responsibility for the hurt she'd caused him. She knew only too well what it felt like to be regarded as nothing more than a friend.

Her phone signaled an incoming text, a reminder from Nan about their one o'clock get-together. Since Amy hadn't returned yet, Tamara left her a note about her whereabouts and gladly set aside the rest of the ranch business for some much-needed girl time.

Chapter 4

Twenty minutes later, Tamara pulled her compact Mitsubishi SUV into a parking space in front of Nan's teashop. Behind her, the fountain centered in the middle of the town square gurgled with a bubbly flow of water. Now that the air hinted of warmer temperatures soon to come, the fountain was only one of the things popping back up after a long, cold winter. Rising above the historic, three story brick buildings, the mountains appeared greener amidst the snow-capped elevations.

Sliding out of her vehicle, she took a deep, appreciative breath as she stepped up on the walk and reached for the door handle. A set of tinkling chimes pealed as she pushed it open and saw Nan standing at one of the quaint, wrought iron tables, talking with a redhead and brunette seated on the matching chairs. All three women looked up, Nan smiling and waving her over.

"There you are. Come and meet Sydney." She nodded to the green-eyed redhead before waving her hand to the other woman peering at Tamara through black-framed glasses. "Avery moved to town a short time after Sydney." The other girl's light brown eyes shone in welcome.

"Hi. Nice to meet you both." Tamara took the empty chair Nan nudged out with her foot.

"Tamara and I go back to grade school together." Nan picked up Sydney's left hand so Tamara could see the sparkling engagement ring. "The rock is from Caden Dunbar. Their engagement is just one thing you've missed since your last visit."

Tamara ignored the reprimand in her friend's voice as she leaned in for a closer look at the ring. "It's beautiful. You must be special if you've tamed Caden." Even before she had witnessed that scene in Connor's barn, she had heard the rumors surrounding the wild Dunbar brothers and their kinky passions. She'd never been able to forget her first and only glimpse of Connor's dominant side, or the interest and vivid dreams it had stirred.

Sydney laughed. "Trust me, Caden is not 'tamed'." She finger-quoted the word tamed. "But I wouldn't want him to be. I fell for him just as he is."

"Well, congratulations," Tamara said, not sure how to respond to that.

Two more customers entered, drawing Nan's attention. "Let me get your orders before I take theirs. Tamara, I have a new apple spice you'll like and that goes good with the apple turnovers fresh from the bakery."

Tamara groaned. "Yes to both, and if I gain weight, I'm not coming back."

"I said that too, but here I am." Avery sighed. "It's a good thing Grayson likes my… curves." She looked down with a rueful grimace.

Nan smiled. "I can't believe you're still blushing and stuttering after being with our sheriff for over two months."

"Really?" Tamara remembered the good-looking, sexy sheriff coming out to the ranch to offer his personal condolences last year and knew he was well liked and respected in the county. She also knew he was included in the gossip surrounding the Dunbar brothers and a secret club the three had opened over six years ago. Before she had left, Nan revealed she'd just become a member and loved everything about the place.

"Her wheels are turning, girlfriends," Nan smirked. "Yes, Tamara knows about The Barn and no, she doesn't swing that way, at least not yet." With that taunting remark, she pivoted and moved behind the glass-encased counter to brew their tea.

"You should know, Tamara, neither of us have been members long and are both new to the…" Avery waved her hand. "The… stuff that goes on there."

Sydney rolled her eyes. "New, yes, compared to Nan. But we're well past the newbie stage, thank goodness. It's much more fun when the inhibitions are stripped away, provided the right person does the stripping. Nan says you've been living in Boise for a few years but grew up here."

Tamara wondered if Sydney sensed how uncomfortable talk about the sex club Connor was part owner of made her. It wasn't the mention of kink that rubbed her the wrong way, but picturing him with a different woman every weekend, indulging in stuff she'd only ever dreamed about since she'd gotten an up-close look at him in action.

"Yes, working as a physical therapist in a rehab, but I missed home," she admitted as Nan returned with three steaming cups and a plate of turnovers.

"Then you shouldn't have stayed away so long," she rebuked her. "I plan on getting you drunk soon so I can pull the real reason you took that job out of you."

"*Ooh*, I wanna join you," Sydney insisted with a wicked grin.

"Me too. I've never had such good friends as Nan and Sydney and if you're included now, Tamara, I say no secrets," Avery piped in, ending with a decisive head nod.

Tamara had no idea what got into her. Maybe it was because

she didn't doubt Nan would do everything in her willpower to pull the truth from her and might succeed in getting her to spill the beans about her guilt over accepting Jeremy's proposal when she'd known her feelings didn't run deep enough to make such a commitment. Or, maybe it was because she couldn't get Connor out of her mind and the mention of kink brought up the memory of that hot scene that had dampened her pussy more than any act of intercourse she'd indulged in before or after that prompted her to blurt out the truth without thought.

"Connor, that's who happened."

"I knew it!" Nan crowed.

Tamara narrowed her eyes as her friend plopped into the empty chair next to her. "You did not."

She smirked. "Hon, you've had the hots for that man since you knew what the hots were. It's not like you hid it."

"Oh, God." Dropping her head into her hands, Tamara groaned. "Was I that obvious?"

Sydney and Avery laughed as Nan quipped, "Afraid so, to everyone but Connor. The man either wore blinders around you or just plain didn't want to go there. He can be as stubborn as you."

She looked up and sighed. "That's the truth."

"What are you going to do?" Avery asked, sipping her tea.

Taking a big bite of the sweet turnover, she didn't have to think about her answer as she said, "Nothing. He made it clear when he was tired of my antics when I was twenty-five that I'm nothing but a friend and I doubt that will change. I need to move on, and I need to do it here because here is where I want to be."

"Near Connor."

She glanced at Sydney and saw the question in her eyes. "Yes. I know he didn't mean his hurtful words and he'll always be my friend. I don't want to lose that connection again."

Slapping her hands down on the table, Nan surprised her by suggesting, "Come to the club. Meet some new people. There are several guys you'll like, and who will be not only good to you but good for you."

Tamara sputtered on a disbelieving laugh. "How am I supposed to move on at such a place? One, I'm not into kink, and two, *he'll* be there."

"Exactly. Show him you have grown up and can do whatever you want, including indulging in the same kinks as him."

"Oh, good idea, Nan," Sydney crooned.

Heat enveloped Tamara as she imagined Connor watching her with someone else, and her interest took hold. What could it hurt to explore the curiosity that had stirred to life the one time she'd watched him? She didn't have to take it far, and what better way to start moving on than with someone who wouldn't expect anything except for her to submit to his wishes for an hour?

But she needed clarification before taking such a big risk with the unknown. "What if I don't want to participate, or I start something with someone and want to stop?"

Avery laid a light hand on her arm. "I fretted over things like that also, but Grayson showed me I was not only safe with him, but free to end things whenever I wanted. It was a heady feeling of power, I've got to admit."

She looked at the three women staring at her with small smiles of expectation and thought, *why the heck not*? Why let Connor, who refused to change, keep her from exploring new things, seeking a new, or several new relationships? They didn't have to lead to anything permanent; she had time to form a committed relationship later, after she worked him out of her system and could settle down with one person without feeling guilty because she wanted someone else more.

Before she could change her mind or think it to death, she reached for a second turnover with a nod. "I'm in, but only to observe, and you three better back me up and be there for me."

"Fuck, yes," Nan beamed.

An hour later, Tamara returned home still grappling with her decision to go as a guest to a BDSM club. Knowing about the place and what went on there and attending as an interested guest were two wildly different things, and she had to admit she would be out of her depth in such a place. So why, she asked herself as the front door opened and she saw Amy waiting for her with a broad smile of welcome, was she planning on going? With a mental headshake, she guessed seeing Connor again, touching him, hearing his voice, had left her more rattled and desperate than ever to get over him.

Putting all her insecurities and doubts aside, she skipped up the porch steps and threw her arms around her stepmother, happy to see her back again. She'd left only a few days after Tamara returned home and they still had a lot of catching up to do. "When did you get in?" Pulling back, Tamara basked in the warmth of Amy's blue eyes and her motherly hug of welcome.

"Only thirty minutes ago. I love my sister, but it's good to be home. How are you, Tammy?"

Amy's nickname for her brought tears to her eyes, as did her embrace. Damn but she'd been on an emotional roller coaster since seeing Connor yesterday, and she didn't like it. "Are you ever going to quit calling me Tammy?"

"Nope." Pulling back, Amy looked her over with a critical eye before ushering her inside. "You look good. How was your visit to town and your first day on the new job?"

"Great. I like everyone at the clinic, and I love the changes Nan's made to her teashop. She introduced me to two newcomers to Willow Springs this afternoon, who are very nice."

"Let me guess," Amy said as Tamara followed her into the kitchen and smelled something wonderful cooking in the oven. "That would be Sydney Greenbriar and Avery Pierce, Caden Dunbar and the sheriff's new girls?"

Laughing, she plopped onto a kitchen chair at the small, round corner table. "I should have known you still keep up with who's who and who's doing what."

"Of course. I've heard they're all members of that club everyone likes to speculate about." Amy shot her a sly glance as she joined Tamara at the table with a glass of tea. "You know, the one Connor Dunbar belongs to."

"Oh, good grief..." Her stepmother thrived on the small-town gossip. Giving her a narrowed eyed, suspicious glare, Tamara knew it wasn't a coincidence she brought up the exact subject she'd just discussed with her friend. "You talked to Nan already."

"Guilty. I just got off the phone with her. She wants my help in making sure you don't change your mind. I think it's a grand idea. Show that man you're not pining for him anymore and won't be sitting around doing nothing now that you're back for good."

Tamara's chest filled with warmth and her eyes grew misty with gratitude and pleasure stemming from the open, honest and supportive relationship she'd always enjoyed with her stepmother. Amy had encouraged her to confide in her as soon as her mother had taken off and made spilling her guts on more than one occasion easy to do, keeping their private 'girl' moments between the two of them. Her father had been wonderful, spoiling her and never stingy with his love and praise, but he was still her father and some things she could never imagine being comfortable enough to discuss with him.

"I'm not going to do anything, just visit, and socialize." She allowed a small smile to curve her lips. "Besides, I think it would be fun to watch," she teased, thinking it wouldn't be the first time she'd indulged in voyeurism. Tamara had never spoken a word to anyone about the scene she'd stumbled upon when riding to Connor's that day, not even to Amy or Nan. Some things were best kept private.

"You're a good girl, hon, always have been. I've known those Dunbar boys, and several others who are members for ages, and trust them to look out for you. So, feel free to be a bad girl for a change. It'll do you good."

TAMARA TURNED onto the highway praying she wasn't making a mistake. *Be a bad girl for a change.* Amy's suggestion had been replaying in her head for the last few days, and each time she'd thought about it, the stronger her desire grew to do just that despite her lingering unsurety. Shifting on the car seat, her bare buttocks tingled under the snug black skirt. It wasn't the first time she'd worn a thong, but always before she'd been dressed to please and seduce Jeremy, each time hoping and praying her response to sex with him would improve. It never did, which was only one of the reasons she'd ended their engagement. Approaching the road off the highway that would take her to the club, she shoved those depressing thoughts aside, gripped the steering wheel tighter and made the turn.

Several bumpy minutes later, the narrow, unpaved lane leading to The Barn ended at a large, tree shrouded copse and gravel parking lot in front of the two-story restored farm structure. Tamara had heard rumors the Dunbars and Sheriff Monroe were partnering in a private club over seven years ago, and that the three of them had all lent a hand in converting an old barn into a gathering place for members to indulge in their kinky preferences. The townsfolk had always accepted the rumors, and likelihood of their truth with good-natured shrugs of indifference. Maybe a few older citizens continued to mumble under their breath, but for the most part, the intrigued speculation outweighed the snide criticism. What judgmental remarks had filtered back to members were brushed aside with unconcern.

Tamara turned off the engine and gazed around at the vehicles, trying to figure out who was already inside by makes and models. She hadn't been back long enough to familiarize herself with certain changes, but she spotted Nan's same sporty Nissan with as much relief as she felt when she didn't see Connor's truck. Maybe he would show up later tonight, but after giving Nan's invitation serious thought the last four days and getting her stepmother's not-so-surprising approval, she'd vowed to enjoy herself regardless of his presence or not.

After sending Nan a text she was here and heading in, she stepped out into the much cooler night air and dashed up to the wide double doors. Ignoring her quivering abdominal muscles, she entered a large foyer and relaxed as Nan came through a door that appeared to lead into a much larger space.

"Hey," she greeted her, shrugging out of her knee-length jacket.

"I'm so glad you didn't change your mind." Nan rushed forward, her long slender legs showcased to perfection in a thigh-skimming sheath that dipped low enough over her breasts to reveal teasing glimpses of pert, dusky nipples.

"How could I with you hounding me with calls and messages every few hours? In here?" She nodded to a large walk-in closet where several other light coats were already hung.

"Yes, and shoes in one of these cubbies." Nan pointed to several rows of open cubicles along one wall and then to the opposite side of the entry. "Over there are the restrooms."

"Good to know," Tamara replied as she stowed her shoes and then ran clammy hands down her sides. "How's this look?" After Nan told her only a Master could waive the dress code requiring bare legs, she'd suggested a skirt to go with the red camisole top she lent her.

"You look fabulous and fill out that top better than me. Come on. Sydney's keeping Master Caden company upstairs while he monitors, but Avery is at the bar with Master Grayson. Remember," Nan added as she reached for the door, "respectful titles or you'll get reprimanded."

"Not spanked?" Tamara meant that as a joke as she entered behind Nan, but her friend turned a serious look on her.

"No, at least not tonight. But you will if you return, which I hope you'll want to do."

A sultry voice crooned to an erotic beat that was somehow fitting for the electric, sexually charged atmosphere Tamara stepped into. Lighting nestled in the overhead rafters shed enough of a glow onto the spacious lower level to make it easy to see everyone and everything. She cast a quick glance toward the low cries and flesh-slapping sounds emanating from the loft, her eyes widening when she could just barely make out the shapes of a few apparatus and the writhing, naked bodies attached to them. She went hot and cold all at once, shivering from the impact of viewing scenes of a lifestyle that had first sparked her curiosity five long years ago.

Nan's giggle drew her attention, her rueful smile prompting Tamara to return the grin. "Am I gawking like the newbie I am?"

"Oh, yeah, and I love it. At least you're not turning tail and running."

"No…" She stumbled to a halt as they came to a table where a man was pressing his hand between the shoulder blades of the woman bent over the back of a chair, his other hand smacking her bare, upturned, wiggling buttocks. "At least, not yet," she muttered in an aside to Nan.

Taking her arm, Nan dragged her away from the scene Tamara found both intriguing and somewhat off-putting. She couldn't imagine enjoying the humiliation of a public chastisement or those harsh swats, but that didn't stop her cheeks from clenching as they wound their way to the bar in the center of the cavernous room. A heated wave of mortification spread up her neck and face as the man she recognized as Sheriff Monroe ran an appreciative gaze down to her breasts and her already turgid nipples puckered even tighter. Without looking down, she knew the thin satin revealed every prominent bump on her areolas and wished Nan had chosen something she could have worn a bra with.

With a quick, guilty glance at Avery, Tamara hopped onto the stool next to her. "Wow, this place is… something," she stated, hunching over as she propped her arms on the bar top.

"Relax, Tamara. Everyone's okay with looking," Master Grayson drawled around the toothpick in his mouth as he winked at Avery.

Avery reddened but smiled back at him. "It takes getting used to, that's for sure. *Sheesh*, I'm still adjusting." She shifted on the seat and a low groan slipped out of her mouth. "And learning Master Grayson's limits."

Nan laughed and remained standing between the two. "You love it as much as I do. Admit it."

"Nan, sugar, no sub here loves discipline as much as you." Grayson handed her a beer as he passed Tamara a drink card. "What can I get you? You're limited to two alcohol drinks a night."

"I'll just stick with a soda, please." She couldn't seem to stop looking around; there was so much going on she wanted to keep her wits about her so as not to miss anything. The dance floor teemed with gyrating bodies, the few women dancing topless appearing comfortable having their partner's hands all over their bouncing flesh. Two padded benches situated on the wall opposite of the dance floor drew her gaze, and she couldn't seem to drag her eyes away from the one occupied by a curvy blonde. Even several feet away she could hear the girl's grunts and see her damp response to the Dom's grinding possession of her ass. "I see what you mean, Avery." Taking the cold Pepsi from Master Grayson, she looked away from his knowing smirk and eased the sudden dryness coating her throat with a long swallow as he moved away to serve someone else.

"How about I give you a tour? We can…" A look of pleasure and excitement flitted across Nan's face and Tamara swiveled to see a tall, light-haired man approaching who looked vaguely familiar.

"Master Dan," Nan purred with a small smile. Her soft voice carried a hint of need Tamara couldn't fail to miss.

"Nan." Holding out his hand in silent invitation, Nan hesitated, looking back at Tamara.

"Thank you, Sir, but I have a guest…"

"Go," Tamara interjected quickly. "Trust me, I'm fine just sitting here, watching."

"Are you sure?"

"I'll stay until Master Grayson's bar tending shift is up," Avery offered.

Nan nodded. "Okay, thanks." Taking Master Dan's hand, she finger-waved, saying, "I'll come find you shortly."

Dan's dark chocolate eyes went to slits. "I don't rush my scenes."

Nervous and embarrassed, Tamara muttered, "Go, shoo. I'm fine. Don't hurry."

"I've seen that man in action and noticed how much he enjoys taking his time," Avery told Tamara as they both watched the other couple climb the stairs to the loft.

"We've been friends for years, but I know very little about her interest in all of this." Tamara waved a hand out. "I do remember her always being in a good mood following a night spent here. He's the lawyer, right?" At the snap of leather on bare skin, her eyes wandered up to the loft again.

Avery nodded. "Yes and was a big help when I returned to Chicago to give my statement against two corrupt cops. I'll tell you more about that later, as I can see your mind is elsewhere."

"Oh, sorry, I was listening but, wow, I can't seem to get over how relaxed everyone is with all that's going on."

The next thirty minutes passed in a blur of names and information as Avery and Grayson introduced her to people and explained the rules. As Tamara's embarrassment eased, she discovered her penchant for voyeurism hadn't been a onetime thing and that she didn't have to participate in a scene to enjoy herself, but curiosity grabbed hold as a dark-haired man strolled up to the bar and gave her a slow smile and appreciative look.

Holding out his hand, he introduced himself. "I'm Master Devin. I haven't seen you in here before."

"I'm Tamara, Nan's guest for the night." She took his hand, enjoying the warm clasp. Tall and lean, his blue eyes reminded her of Connor, but she quickly shoved thoughts of him aside, as she'd been doing since she'd arrived.

"Where's Greg tonight?" Grayson asked as he returned.

"Still with Connor looking at a pair of fillies we're thinking of adding to our stables." Turning back to Tamara, Devin asked, "Have you explored what we have to offer here yet?"

She flicked a glance at Avery who just smiled in return, leaving it up to her to decide. "Uh, no, but…"

"Good. Come with me and I'll show you around. You can let me know if anything interests you enough to try."

Grayson nodded. "Go ahead, Tamara. You can trust Master Devin, and anyone else here."

Curiosity and a need to keep her mind off Connor prompted Tamara to take his hand again before she could change her mind. "Thank you."

"My pleasure. Let's go upstairs. Feel free to ask any questions."

Devin led her toward the stairs, pausing when she halted and gaped at the couple enjoying a huge open shower, the marbled former stall big enough to hold six people. With her arms restrained above her, the petite brunette released a sigh of pleasure as multiple pelting sprays dampened her swaying body. The man behind her looked just as sexy as he pulled her hips back and thrust inside her with a low grunt.

"This is the newest addition to the club. It's only been in use now for two weeks." Devin's small smile widened when she couldn't seem to look away from the erotic scene.

Shaking her head, she muttered, "You can't be shy around here, can you?"

"Most people aren't after a visit or two," he replied with a tug on her hand.

Tamara couldn't help it. A picture of herself in place of the brunette with Connor being the one plowing into her with rigorous plunges filled her head. Thank goodness he wasn't here, or she might not have gotten up the gumption to follow Master Devin up the stairs. If she thought the shower scene was eye-boggling and stirring, that was nothing compared to what was happening on some odd contraptions in the loft. She appreciated the way Master Devin kept hold of her hand as he showed her around, his grip as warm and supportive as his low voice.

"Have you met Master Brett and his wife, Sue Ellen?" he asked after she shied away from a corner swing when she saw Nan spread-eagle on it. She wasn't quite ready to see so much of her best friend, especially after catching a glimpse of her denuded mons.

"No, at least I don't think so."

Ushering her over to a wood-slatted A frame, he bent and whispered in her ear, "Don't speak unless invited to, in case someone hasn't mentioned that rule to you yet."

"Grayson… I mean Master Grayson did," she amended when he frowned. Turning her attention to the married couple, she could barely make out the red lines crisscrossing Sue Ellen's torso, waist and thighs in the dim lighting but the contentment and sated glow in the woman's eyes as she gazed at her husband was unmistakable. A shudder ran through Tamara as she imagined being bound naked against the wood frame and her body broke out in a light sweat.

A soft cry drew her head around in time to watch Sydney fall into Caden's arms as he released her from a dangling chain, her slender body gleaming and shaking as she burrowed against his wide chest. The soft look on her fiancé's face as he stroked a hand down her bare back and over her buttocks caused Tamara's chest to constrict. She'd longed for just such a look from Connor, as well as his touch for ten years.

Sydney opened her eyes and saw them approaching, her smile widening. "Are you having fun?"

"Yes, when I'm not feeling out of my element and like I'm sticking out like the inexperienced guest I am," she admitted.

Caden lifted one dark brown brow. "It's good to see you again, Tamara. I'm sure Master Devin will be more than happy to tutor you, if you want to try out something."

"More than happy. I've been letting her set the pace. The possibilities are endless on this apparatus." Devin pointed to a large suspended wagon wheel and the smaller one off to the side.

Sydney giggled and sent Caden a sly look. "I have a fond memory of the wheel."

Caden responded with a sharp smack on her butt. "You have a fond memory of enjoying the undivided attention of two men."

"True." Sydney leaned against him, including Tamara in her smile.

Tamara caught Caden's indulgent glance, the same tender look she'd seen reflected on other Dom's faces tonight as they tormented the woman they'd partnered with. It didn't seem to matter if it was someone they'd hooked up with for the night or, like her friends and the married couple, Master Brett and Sue Ellen, a committed couple. The men all appeared intent on two things: being in charge and seeing to their subs needs, whatever they might be. Everyone was so at ease with each other, the Doms comfortable with their roles, the women with their orders and the vulnerability of their nakedness, like Sydney portrayed. A curl of envy and a desire to reach that same level of contentment made her stomach muscles clutch.

"The smaller wheel offers different suggestions," Devin said, gazing at her with an intent expression. "Want to spin it and try whatever it lands on?" All three laughed at whatever unease they must have seen on her face before he rushed to assure her. "Relax, I was just teasing you. If you want to try bondage – no touching – I suggest one of the benches."

Did she want to? As she thought about it, Connor's hurtful words and how they had sent her running away from everything and everyone she loved flitted through her head. Why shouldn't she appease her curiosity? Tonight would be the time to explore the itch watching him all those years ago had generated since he wasn't here to interrupt and cause her grief. And maybe something new, something different was what she needed to spice up her life and keep her from pining for him.

"I think I would like to," she finally answered, grateful for his patient silence as she worked out her decision.

"That's a girl. Let's go downstairs. The two up here are occupied and if we wait, you might change your mind, and that would be a shame."

Sydney gave her a nod of encouragement and Tamara turned to follow Master Devin's long-legged stride, her pulse jumping with both excitement and nerves.

Chapter 5

Connor followed his friend and now business partner into the parking lot of The Barn with little enthusiasm for socializing. Working out a deal with Greg on the purchase of several horses for trail rides at his and Devin's dude ranch added to the perk of having Tam back in his life, even if he was unsure about how to define their relationship now. That one uncertainty had a lot to do with his lack of interest in coming out to the club tonight. He'd been itching to see her again, just to spend time with her and catch up on everything she'd been doing the past few years but didn't want to push his luck since their relationship remained tenuous. She'd always had a way of keeping him tied up in knots, but in the past, he figured those knots were due to the scrapes he'd been around to help her out of. Now, his only explanation for what was causing them was the uncertainty of where he stood with her.

Greg beat him to the front door and pulled it open, raising a brow in inquiry as he said, "That frown is going to keep the subs at bay."

"No it won't. They like me no matter what my mood is," he replied with a wry grin as he entered before Greg. Faint strains of edgy music seeped through the closed doors to the playroom, along with the hum of low voices. His pulse kicked up a notch as the two of them stepped into the cavernous space and he could now catch the high-pitched cries coming from happily tormented subs.

"Christ, I love this place," Greg murmured on a deep inhale that lifted his wide shoulders. "I think I'll track down my partner and see who's willing to turn themselves over to the two of us."

Connor's grin widened. Greg and his longtime friend, Devin were new to The Barn but already enjoyed their reputation of preferring ménages. "Go on," he encouraged with a nod. "I want to start with a drink."

With a slap on Connor's back, Greg sauntered off and Connor headed toward the bar. He spotted Caden bar tending and decided to take over for his brother early instead of waiting for his assigned time slot. He wasn't in the mood yet to hook up with anyone. But his intended offer slid to the backburner as his roaming gaze landed on a spanking bench at the back of the room and he went rigid in disbelief. Slamming to a stunned halt as he reached the bar, he took a moment to confirm it was Tam's slender, toned body draped over the apparatus, her long black braid hanging over her shoulder and her smooth limbs bound in leather cuffs.

Disbelief morphed into anger, his defense against the kernel of lust that gripped him, just like when he'd caught her spying on him. *Wrong, that's just plain wrong*, he couldn't help thinking. Tam, *his* Tam had no business being in his club. This was the young girl he'd taught to ride, the teenager he'd given driving lessons to and stood up for against her randy prom date. The same young woman he had cheered on at jumping competitions and praised for earning a college scholarship. The echo of her laughter reaching his ears from across the fields as she rode with carefree abandonment resonated in his head. That innocent, exuberant girl had no business bending over a spanking bench with her tight black skirt hiked up enough to reveal the sweet under curve of her buttocks.

Connor took two steps forward, intending to lay into both her and Devin and stop them before either could take whatever they were doing one step further, but found his path blocked by his brother's large frame and scowl. "Get out of my way," he snapped, his jaw tightening with frustration.

"Take a deep breath and think, Connor. She's here as Nan's guest and isn't complaining. I should know as I've been keeping a close eye on her. Devin is just showing her the ropes." Caden's gaze turned sympathetic. "She's not a kid anymore. Didn't you learn that when she took off?"

Caden's words hit him as sharply as a slap in the face. Knowing him better than anyone else, his only sibling had guessed correctly that the cause of Connor's sour mood following Tam's departure to Boise had something to do with her decision. He'd told no one, not even Caden about what happened at his stable that morning, but Caden had always enjoyed ribbing him about his close relationship and attachment to Tam and easily put two and two together, guessing they'd had a falling out.

Bracing his hands on his hips, he bent slightly at the waist and sucked in a deep breath. "Fuck, you're right." He couldn't get angry with her again. The last time he'd blown up at her he admitted to being unprepared for seeing the desire reflected in her pewter eyes and on her flushed face. And nothing could have prepared him for the blunt force trauma of his instant, lustful response that had caught him off guard and without the shield he usually erected to keep from acknowledging her as a grown woman. He couldn't lose her again, but sure as hell couldn't stand by and watch her submit to masterful men he shared close ties to. Their demands would taint the fresh innocence that didn't belong here, and he said as much to Caden.

"She doesn't belong here, she's not submissive and… fuck it, Caden, we both watched her grow up."

Caden nodded. "Yes, but she *has* grown up and from the hint of excitement and curiosity I've seen on her face, she may have a streak of submissiveness. She's certainly exhibited enough interest and courage to give bondage a try."

One thing Tam didn't lack was courage. "Fine. I'll just talk to her." Remembering the past, this time he prepared himself for whatever level of lust she might reveal when she saw him. Greg must have spotted Devin just then because Connor intercepted him before he could reach his best friend. "Wait up, will you? She's a friend of mine. I want to talk to her."

"Sure, no problem."

"Thanks." There was no way, no matter what Tam said, that he would let her indulge in a ménage tonight, not here where he would have no choice but to keep watch. With relief, he noticed Devin reaching down to her ankles to remove the cuffs as he approached. "Here, let me help," he offered, moving to the side and reaching for her bound right wrist. He saw her jerk and then stiffen right before her head whipped up and she looked at him with round eyes filled with the same light of sexual awareness and need as the day he'd driven her away. *Shit.*

HEIGHTENED sexual awareness drew goosebumps along Tamara's arms even as a slow, steady flow of warmth invaded her body upon hearing Connor's voice. Her buttocks clenched as she imagined those blue eyes peeking at the lower part of her exposed butt. A frisson of unease had rippled down her spine when Master Devin first restrained her, but the longer she lay there with his hand running down her back in soothing strokes, the more relaxed she'd become. It was when he'd slid his palm down to her bare thigh and squeezed, asking her if she'd like to go a step further, that she'd balked. He hadn't hesitated to remove his hand and reach to free her ankle, and she'd been contemplating whether to leave or return to the bar to continue watching when Connor's sudden appearance delivered a jolting electric zap that puckered her nipples and dampened her pussy.

"I thought you weren't coming tonight," she managed to say as he helped her up and wrapped an arm around her when she wobbled. She didn't mention her unsteady legs resulted from his presence instead of her first experience with sexual bondage.

"Well you thought wrong. We need to talk." With a jerk of his head, he indicated the sliding doors leading to a back deck. "In private. First, thank Master Devin for his time."

The touch of hardness he had injected into his light tone made her toes curl. Thank goodness what she could see of his face under the black Stetson remained calm and friendly. She didn't want to fight with him, but she'd also decided she wasn't ready to leave. Looking up at the other man, she smiled in gratitude. He'd been very nice and accommodating.

"Thank you, Master Devin." Waving at the bench, she added, "It was different, in a strange way, but not off-putting."

"Honest and pretty." Devin bent down and brushed his mouth over hers. "If you return and want to try something else, look me up." With a nod and knowing smile toward Connor, he pivoted and joined the man waiting several feet away.

"That was nice of him," she said as Connor tugged her toward the doors.

Sliding one open, he ushered her outside with a hand on her lower back. "He's not nice. No one here is nice. You need to remember that."

As soon as he closed the door, she moved away from him, finding it too hard to concentrate if they were touching. The bubbling hot tub looked appealing, but she doubted she would get a chance to try it out any time soon. Crossing her arms, she leaned against the wood rail with a sigh. "I disagree. Connor, are we going to fight?"

Reaching out, he tugged on her hair with a familiar, indulgent smile that helped ease her tension. "No, little one. Caden pointed out you're a grown woman, and an invited guest. But you don't belong here. You're way too… naïve for what goes on in this place and do not understand what you're subjecting yourself to. You need to go home."

His gentle tone unnerved Tamara. "Little one?" He'd never called her that before.

Connor shrugged. "You don't want me to call you sweetie."

No, she didn't. Narrowing her eyes, she cut to the chase. "Like I and now others keep reminding you, I am not a kid anymore."

"But you're also not wise about kinky sex, admit it," he returned in a cooler tone.

"Devin gave me a tour and explained a lot."

"*Master* Devin, and here I'm Master Connor, regardless of our friendship. I just can't imagine you bending to the will of a Master and don't want to see you hurt. I've never wanted that. Go home, Tam," he whispered, running one finger down her cheek.

Tears pricked her eyes. Not because he was being mean, like the last time, but because he wasn't. He kept his tone reasonable, choosing his words with care, and yet they still cut her to the bone. He refused to step out of his over-protective friend role and regard her as someone capable of thinking for herself when her decisions involved her sexual cravings. Her first inclination was to politely refuse and return to watching and socializing, but her desire to do so had waned and now she wanted to distance herself from the man she continued to want but couldn't have.

"Excuse me, *Master* Connor. I want to speak with Nan." She sidled around him, surprised when he didn't stop her.

Tamara heard his frustrated muttering as she went back inside and came close to smiling until she spotted her friend sitting on Master Dan's lap, a look of pure, sated bliss etched on her face. As she neared their table, she noticed the red stripes decorating the fullness of her friend's breasts and the top of her thighs, guessing her bottom bore matching lines from the way Nan kept fidgeting. She slowed her steps, rethinking her intention to whine to Nan and then take off. It wouldn't be right to dim another's pleasure because Connor succeeded in dampening hers. Yeah, she needed to go and do some serious thinking before deciding her next move toward pursuing this growing passion for a lifestyle that had intrigued her for years.

"Hey, girlfriend. How's it going?" Nan tilted her head, giving Tamara a speculative look.

"Good, real good in fact. Uh, Master Devin showed me around and I even got up the nerve to let him tie me down. But I'm going to head home now. I need a little breathing room, and time to take all this in." She looked around the room.

"I understand. Let me slip something on and I'll walk out with you."

Tamara waved her back down. Dan had released her but didn't look happy about it. "Don't be silly. This place is safe, inside and out, isn't it?" She posed her question to the lawyer whose dark gaze was as unnerving as every other Dom in this place.

"Of course it is, but there is always the chance of someone lurking outside. I'll walk you out," Connor said from behind her as he grasped her elbow. "Let's go."

"Eager to get rid of me?" she quipped as he wasted no time escorting her into the foyer.

"No, just wanting to ensure you're okay, and that we're good."

Ignoring that statement, she pulled from his warm clasp and retrieved her shoes and jacket, remaining silent until they reached her vehicle. Opening the door, she slid behind the wheel and looked up at him. Shrouded in darkness, his tall, imposing figure would have appeared intimidating if she didn't know him so well. "We're good, Con, but that doesn't mean I've agreed to not come back. I want to think about it. Goodnight." Taking advantage of his surprise, she yanked the door shut and drove away without looking back.

Connor stood for a moment, swearing under his breath, digging his keys out of his pocket and striding to his truck. Those knots Tam was so good at tying him up in had returned and he needed to figure out how to loosen them without driving her away again.

PULLING into the drive in front of the house, Tamara spotted the glowing orange tip of a cigarette from across the wide lawn between her and the stable. Hopping out of her vehicle, she dashed over and recognized the new hire, Neil, leaning against the wood building as if he didn't realize the stupidity and carelessness of his smoking.

"Neil, right? I'm sorry, we don't allow smoking anywhere on the ranch. It's too easy to toss a burning stub onto dry timber or grass. Put it out, please." It was difficult to keep her irritation in check.

"Who the hell are you?" he drawled, blatant insolence portrayed in his voice and stance.

Stiffening against the rude comeback, she bit back the urge to fire him on the spot, giving him the benefit of the doubt he was just reacting to a stranger's reprimand. "I'm the owner of this spread and your boss."

"*Shit.*" He straightened and crushed the bud beneath his boot. "Sorry. It's been a rough day."

She nodded. "Jason mentioned you're still learning the ropes, and I'm good with that, but please don't speak that way to anyone here. We're like family, one I hope you'll learn to be a part of. Goodnight." Pivoting, she heard him return her goodnight as she headed back up to the house.

Tamara entered the darkened entry, putting that unpleasant incident out of her mind as she went straight to the kitchen. Flipping on the under counter lights, she opened the freezer and pulled out a carton of Rocky Road ice cream. Grabbing a spoon, she sat at the table and dug in, her mind continuing to whirl with everything she'd seen at the club, her surprising response to bondage and her not-so-surprising reaction to Connor. Most times, she didn't know whether to drop to her knees and beg him to change his mind about expanding their relationship or to smack him upside the head for being so rigid.

"Stubborn moron," she muttered around a mouthful of cold chocolate.

"Uh, oh. It didn't go well." Amy shuffled into the kitchen wearing a robe and concerned look.

"What gave it away?" Tamara groused.

"You only stuff your face with ice cream when you're upset or mad. Share that and tell me what happened." After getting a spoon, her stepmother joined her at the table and Tamara pushed the carton between them.

Shrugging, she gave Amy an honest answer. "Not much. One of the members, a nice guy, showed me around. It was embarrassing at first, but you can't help getting turned on." Fanning herself, she grinned at the woman she'd always felt comfortable talking to. "Hot with a capital H."

"I'll take your word for it since I have no interest in that lifestyle. Thinking about getting involved with someone else has been difficult enough. I still miss your dad. I take it Connor showed up." Amy indulged in a large scoop as she kept her gaze on Tamara.

"I still miss him too, and yes, Con was there." Tamara sighed, envying Amy a relationship she despaired of ever having. Shoving aside her melancholy, she told her about Connor's continued obstinance. "I want to go back, but honestly, Amy, I only want to explore further with him." Dropping her head into her hands, she groaned, "What am I going to do?"

"I can't tell you that, but my advice is to stop letting him dictate your life, as hard as that might be."

Tamara set her spoon down and looked up again. "You know, you're right. No matter how many trips back here I made when I was living in Boise, it wasn't the same. I missed seeing you and Dad every day, and Galahad, all because of him." She didn't mention her failed relationship with Jeremy, or the guilt she still harbored from leading him on for far too long. All she'd told anyone was that it hadn't worked out and she intended that to be all she revealed. Some mistakes were best kept private. "I'm going back to the club and damn it, I will have fun without him." She gave a decisive nod, as if sealing her decision.

"Good for you, sweetheart. Now, let's polish this off and get to bed. I'm tired."

"First, tell me about you and Jason," she insisted, wanting Amy's happiness.

Amy shifted her eyes away and then returned her gaze to Tamara. "I like him. How much, I haven't decided yet."

"Good. You deserve to find someone else. And," her grin turned wicked, "he's *hawt*."

They both giggled like teenagers as Amy stuttered, "Yeah… he is that."

The first thing Tamara did the next morning was place a call to Nan, asking her how much it cost to join the club and what she had to do before she could change her mind or think the decision to death. After expressing her approval, Nan passed on the website where she filled out the application. Given the high cost of a year's membership and her uncertainty over how far she was inclined to go, she opted for the more affordable one month's entry fee to start with.

With a light step over making that decision, she skipped out to the barn and saddled Galahad. "Good morning, big guy," she crooned to the fourteen-year-old stallion. She could still recall the exaltation that had swept through her when her dad and stepmother presented the Arabian colt to her on her sixteenth birthday. She'd been competing in jumping competitions for three years and had been considered a top teen contender. Her excitement over the chance to raise and train a horse all on her own had known no bounds. But Galahad was also a prime herding equine and this morning they needed to check the herd before they could play.

Leading him out into the sun, she swung up into the saddle but paused before riding out as Jason rode up with Mark, his right-hand man, both wearing grim expressions. "What's up?"

Frustration tightened his lined face. "We lost two head out of the west pasture last night to the rustlers. I haven't heard if they hit anyone else."

"Was anyone on watch?" With as few employees as they had, it was hard to have someone watching each pasture twenty-four-seven.

Mark scowled. "Neil was supposed to but apparently left early, not feeling well."

Tamara wondered if her lecture on smoking the night before prompted Neil to cut out early. It was getting more difficult each day to cut the new guy some slack. "I guess that can't be helped. At this rate, we'll go broke before the end of summer. I'll do a head count on the herd in the north end. Will you contact the sheriff?" she asked, ready to relieve some of her tension over this news with a long, fast ride. Galahad shifted under her, as if he too found the thieves continued pilfering upsetting.

"Will do," her foreman replied, tipping his hat. Jason swung around with ease, proving he could sit a saddle as well as any of the younger employees. She'd seen him eying Amy from afar since she'd been back, more than a hint of interest in his blue gaze. Amy tried to hide her interest, but Tamara had caught her returning that look and wondered how long the two of them would continue to dance around each other. If anyone deserved a second chance at happiness, it was her stepmother.

Tamara waved to Mark and prodded Galahad into a gallop, the cool morning breeze stimulating her as much as the feel of her steed's powerful muscles bunching under her. She didn't slow until they reached the rest of her small stock. A quick count tallied correctly, offering a touch of relief. At an estimated eight to ten-thousand-dollars a head, she couldn't afford to lose any more.

Pulling the reins, she veered Galahad toward the fence, both of them now eager for playtime. "Come on, boy. This one's a piece of cake." With a nudge to his side, he took off and her whoop of success as he took her over the wood rails with flying ease resonated in the air. Just as they landed on solid ground on the other side, she caught wind of another galloping horse and looked behind her to see Connor trotting up on his Palomino, a wide grin splitting his rugged, tanned face. Her heart leaped before she could control her response to seeing him. Nothing she'd tried managed to put a dent in her desire for the man.

His teeth shone bright white against his swarthy skin and the sexy bristles covering the lower half of his face. With his sun-streaked brown hair pulled back in a leather tie, his wicked blue eyes mere slits under the brim of his Stetson and his arm and leg muscles rippling as he pulled up on his horse, was it any wonder he could have any woman he wanted, in or out of his club?

"You've still got it, little one," he praised her as he drew alongside and they set out at an easy trot with the comfort and ease of old times.

"Of course," she boasted with a laugh and toss of her head, refusing to let him see how pathetic she was over him. "My guy and I are a match made in heaven." Thank goodness he seemed to be in his usual, affable mood. After last night, she wasn't sure what his attitude would be when they saw each other again. He hadn't been happy with her, that had been clear.

"I agree." Connor's eyes turned serious as he said, "I just heard you got hit. I'm sorry. Everyone's stayed vigilant about going after these bastards, but so far, they've proven damn elusive. Grayson is wondering if they have an inside man at one of the ranches."

"That would explain how they can elude the sentries everyone is posting. Unfortunately, our guy was sick last night. I hope they get caught soon. My resources aren't anywhere near yours."

"I know, Tam." He reached over and squeezed her shoulder. "Don't worry, the Dunbar ranch, as well as several others will help in any way we can. Your dad was well liked and highly respected. He'd want us to look out for you."

Tamara swallowed her disappointment. She didn't want him 'looking out for her', as always, no matter the reason. Apparently, she craved the impossible; for him to regard her as more than a neighbor, a friend or the kid he'd befriended. "Thanks, but my few employees are loyal and diligent. We can pull our own weight, one way or another." To take her mind off what she couldn't have, she flipped him a taunting grin and said, "Race you," before taking off.

She heard his laughing shout and the thunder of his horse's hooves as he caught up with her. Side by side, they traversed the wide-open meadow at a ground-eating pace. Her pleasure in the run and the company lightened her mood by the time they neared the line separating their ranches. Panting, she reined in Galahad and beamed at Connor.

"I won!"

"Did not, but I'll give it to you anyway." With a wink, he lowered his hat and turned toward his spread. Waving, he called back, "See you at the clinic tomorrow, kid."

Muttering, "I'll show you next weekend I'm not a kid," she returned to the house to attend the chores waiting for her there.

CONNOR STOPPED BY CADEN'S, whose house sat on the same acreage as their barns, on his way in for therapy Monday morning. The two of them had taken over the thirty-thousand-acre Dunbar spread when their parents retired and moved into a condo in Billings but kept separate homes as they each valued their privacy. They kept their dad in the loop concerning the business side of ranching, but Connor and Caden had cut their eyeteeth on running a ranch and he trusted them to know what they were doing.

His lifted spirits after riding with Tam yesterday still remained, and he was looking forward to seeing her again, even to the annoying workout she would put him through. God, he'd missed hanging out with her, seeing her, talking to her, hearing that infectious laugh of sheer pleasure. Every time he'd caught a glimpse of her or heard through the grapevine she had returned for a visit and he'd visited with Richard to ease his mind by ensuring she was doing well he would leave missing her all over again. He never should have let her avoid talking to him for so long.

The only thing keeping their relationship from getting back to normal was the uncertainty of whether she would insist on returning to the club. As long as that was a possibility their bond would remain fragile. But he refused to mar what looked like a beautiful day emerging with a cloudless blue sky and warmer weather by fretting over whether she would prove as stubborn about that disagreement as with others they'd had.

"Where are you headed?" Caden greeted him as he came out of the house and walked down the drive to lean his arms on the open passenger window of Connor's truck.

"Therapy." Rotating his shoulder, he felt a twinge, but it had improved since he'd been doing the stretches Tam had given him. "It's getting better, slowly."

"Good. If you're up to it, we could use an extra hand branding. We've got calves running around unmarked."

"I know, and that's not good. With the meat packers and auction houses on alert for stolen brands, we need to get them tagged. I can handle it. I'll be back shortly."

Caden gave him a knowing look. "You weren't happy with your therapist the other night."

Blowing out a breath, he tightened his hands on the steering wheel as he recalled seeing Tam restrained over the spanking bench and his uncontrollable reaction to her. "No, as you well know. I still say she had no business being there. She's too young, too naïve and innocent for our lifestyle."

"Yeah, you keep telling yourself that, Con," Caden returned with a derisive curl of his lips. "In the meantime, she's joined and paid a month's fees."

"What? She's planning on returning?" He jerked as if struck. "Stubborn minx," he growled, wondering how much of her decision had to do with genuine interest as opposed to a way to get back at him.

Caden chuckled. "You should see your face."

"I don't have to. Shit." He sighed with frustration. "What am I going to do with her?"

Shaking his head, his brother backed away from the truck. "Oh, no. I'm not helping you with this one. You're on your own unless you screw it up again. Later."

"You wouldn't be getting hitched if it wasn't for me!" Connor called out as Caden strolled toward the barns.

Lifting his hand in acknowledgement, he admitted without turning, "There is that. Good luck."

Putting the truck in gear, Connor pulled away, still baffled by how happy and content Caden acted over the end of his bachelorhood. He'd never dreamed pushing him toward Sydney would lead to a commitment but had to admit they were well suited.

Shifting gears, he turned his mind to another relationship and the dilemma over what to do about it.

By the time he pulled into the clinic's parking lot, Connor had decided he needed to take one more shot at gently steering Tam away from the club. If reasoning didn't work, maybe a hint of what she thought she wanted would be enough to deter her from pushing forward. She hadn't taken it past bondage the other night and he didn't doubt she would have backed off if things had gone further and someone had given her a taste of the discipline side of BDSM. He didn't want her hurt, or even disillusioned, just safely away from his proclivities and their comfortable relationship back on track.

Given the setting, he'd have to keep it quick and simple, but he was good at improvising and even better at getting his point across with a small demonstration that needed few words if she wouldn't listen to reason. Either way, he couldn't risk seeing her at The Barn again. His resolve to keep their relationship platonic, thus preserving their bond, wouldn't hold out.

Chapter 6

Tamara looked up as the door to the PT room opened, this time prepared for seeing Connor again, unlike yesterday when he'd ridden up unexpectedly and joined her on a run just like old times. Her response was the same, a quick rush of pleasure and a jump in her pulse. But being prepared meant she could handle it without letting him know how easily he got to her with his presence and from one look.

With her decision to return to the club made and sealed with payment of a month's fees, she needed to work on keeping her feelings in check around him. It would be a waste of time and money if she couldn't concentrate on exploring and enjoying her newfound interest in what she'd seen going on there because he was nearby.

"Good morning." She greeted him with a smile, rising from behind her desk. Connor removed his hat, placing it on a hook before turning that enigmatic gaze on her. His smile warmed her blood but the look in those eyes as he approached drew a ripple of unease down her spine. "What?" she asked as he reached her and just stood there, his look assessing.

"After all these years, I didn't think there was anything you could do that would surprise me. I was wrong."

She had to harden herself against the way his deep voice and slow drawl washed over her. "You talked to Caden. I never said I wouldn't return to the club, Con, only that I would think about it. I did, and decided I'm interested enough to keep exploring. Now," she said, her tone turning brusque as she set aside her reaction to his nearness. "Have a seat on the mat and I'll do range of motion on your shoulder to see if you did your homework."

She expected more of an argument about the club, but all he said was, "Sure," before sauntering over to the raised mat. Tamara couldn't help admiring his tight butt showcased in snug denim or recalling the way those taut buttocks clenched as he had driven himself into the woman in his barn.

Sitting down, Connor looked up at her with a wicked grin and spread his muscled thighs. Grasping her hips, he pulled her to stand between his legs, the warmth of his large, rough hands seeping through the thin cotton of her medical uniform pants. "You can get an easier grip and range standing here." Releasing his hold, he held out his arm. "Tell me why you're insisting on coming to The Barn. You've never displayed a submissive tendency before. In fact, you're excellent at giving back as good as you get, or, at least you used to be."

Until I saw the focused look on your face and your partner's sated, contented expression when you had finished with her. Tamara knew better than to reveal that thought aloud. Instead, she maneuvered his arm up and down, back and forth as she replied with a careless shrug, "We haven't seen each other in a while and I've changed. Besides, that's not something a person would know until they're confronted with the possibility. You've done well; you're much looser this week."

"You're the one who refused to speak to me for so long. Tam, that lifestyle isn't for you," he returned, his gentle voice and the fondness reflected in his eyes coming close to unraveling her.

"You don't know that, and neither do I. I'm curious and want to find out. Come on." Letting go of his arm, she stepped back before he could touch her again. She would be defenseless against both that look and his hands on her. "I think you can handle an increase in weight, as well as repetitions on the pulleys." She heard his sigh but when he didn't comment further, she hoped that would be the end of it.

"I can handle that. The question is," he stated as he took hold of the pulley and went to work, "can you handle what the Doms want to dish out? I don't think so, and I don't want to see you hurt, and I'm talking about emotionally. No one there would cause you intentional, physical pain." He gave her a wry smile. "Unless you want them to, that is."

"I'm a big girl, but thanks for caring, and for warning me." She turned her back on him and the way his jaw went taut and his eyes flashed with frustration. He'd always had a knack for coaxing her into behaving herself, but she refused to cave to his cajoling this time. His sudden nearness as he came up behind her and spun her around caught her by surprise and her heart pounded with sudden expectation.

Exasperation flashed in his eyes. "Damn it, Tam, I doubt you've ever even been spanked."

"I might have been if you hadn't interrupted me the other night," she shot back, equally frustrated with his obstinance, no matter that it stemmed from caring and concern.

"Really?" A calculated gleam entered his eyes as he ran his hands down her arms in what she could have sworn was a caress designed to soothe. Whatever it was, she enjoyed the light touch. "Well, since it was my fault you didn't get to experience that aspect of BDSM, let me make up for it."

Before she realized his intention, he grabbed her hand and tugged her over to the desk, maneuvering her in front of him.

With a hand between her shoulders, he pressed gently, bending to whisper in her ear. "Lean on the desk. Show me you're willing to experiment with this side of my lifestyle."

His warm breath fanned the side of her neck, raising the tiny hairs on her nape, his words conjuring up all kinds of scenarios. Her voice shook as she whispered, "We're not at the club. This is where I work, where someone might come in." The next appointment wasn't for an hour but that didn't mean someone else couldn't pop in. The very thought sent a flare of heat up her core. When had she become such a pervert? The silent question accompanied her descent over the desk as she braced on her forearms, her only thought to show him how serious she was about continuing with her submissive education. His sudden indrawn breath followed with the brush of his palm over her buttocks. She trembled, thinking maybe it was just Connor who turned her into a promiscuous deviant wannabe.

"Why do you have to be so stubborn?" he bemoaned as he palmed her right cheek. "This is wrong in so many ways, I can't even begin to count. Remember, this is your doing."

The sudden impact of Connor's hand smacking her bottom jarred Tamara into an acute awareness of the minor discomfort, and how it seemed to feed the lust she harbored for him. Another spank followed the first, this one on her opposite cheek, delivered with a touch more force. She jerked, a small whimper escaping at the startling warmth spreading across her backside.

"This is just a taste of what subs are subjected to if they agree to play with a Dom." Two more swats, each a little harder, jiggled her buttocks and built on the heat now expanding from her butt up between her quaking thighs. "Think long and hard, little one, because trust me, I'm being very," *smack*! "very," *smack*! "nice." He ended the teasing torment with an almost casual exploration of her cheeks and then squeezed each throbbing globe, the tight grip emphasizing the ache and stirring her arousal.

Shaken, Tamara tried to lean back against Connor as he helped her straighten, but he shifted away too fast, leaving his hands on her upper arms until she steadied and turned to face him. With her face burning, her heartbeat thumping like a crazed bat and her warmed buttocks pulsing softly, she knew her face reflected the desire she couldn't deny.

Connor dropped his hands as if burned and stumbled back a step, shaking his head. "You're impossible. I've got to run. We'll talk later." Without another word or backward glance, he pivoted, snatched his hat off the hook and dashed out as if the hounds of Hell were after him.

"*I'm* impossible?" she muttered in frustration, ready to pull her hair out over the blind spot he refused to look past. If he thought that little demonstration would deter her, she'd give him something else to think about. If anything, her response reinforced her determination to move forward without him, one way or another. It also left her wondering how much more potent those swats would have been if delivered on her naked flesh.

CONNOR DROVE AWAY from the clinic trying to erase the image of Tam bent over, those taut buttocks softening under his hand, surprising him yet again with her acceptance of a new kink. How was he supposed to keep her at arm's length and save their friendship if she continued to respond as expected of a true submissive? He was beginning to wish she'd stayed in Boise. A pang clutched his chest at that thought, and he knew it wasn't true.

Immersing himself in hard, sweaty work was what he needed to distract him from the difficult position Tam put him in. Branding was already underway by the time he returned to the ranch and made his way to the largest cattle barn. Behind it, the attached corral was teeming with activity, ranch hands and distressed calves making enough noise to wake the dead. Without giving it a second thought, he bounded over the rail and jumped in to help one of the younger hands wrestle a young male to the ground. He barely missed getting kicked by flailing hooves before he and Tyler managed to get the legs lassoed together.

Heart pounding with a surge of adrenaline, he jumped to his feet, snatching his hat off the ground. Slapping the dust from it against his thigh, he grinned at Tyler's red, frustrated face. "You just have to show 'em who's boss, Ty. Don't be afraid to get rough, you won't hurt them." As soon as the words were out of his mouth, Connor realized how appropriate they were for his situation with Tam. Maybe taking her in hand at the club would be the quickest, and safest way to subdue her interest.

"Got it, Boss. I came on right after branding season last year, so I'm still learning the ropes with it. I'll let the blacksmith know we have another ready."

Tyler gave him a two-fingered salute before jogging into the barn. Connor bent down and ran his hand over the stressed calf's head. "You're okay, little fellow." The Dunbar Ranch had switched to the more humane method of using liquid nitrogen to cool a branding iron before applying it to a flank and altering the hair follicles. The whitened fur would be in the shape of a D, labeling the animal as their property and making it harder for thieves to unload their stolen cattle.

"No wonder all the girls have been missing your attention," Grayson said from behind Connor.

Strolling over to the fence, Connor leaned his arms on the top rail next to the sheriff's. "What brings you out here today?" he asked, ignoring Grayson's reference to his bouts of celibacy in the past few months.

"I wanted to let you know we have a bead on the rustlers. Law enforcement in the next county came across an abandoned trailer." Grayson's eyes turned flinty as he ground out, "Bastards crammed twelve head into a trailer only big enough to hold six, maybe seven. Four dead, two more likely to be. They abandoned the haul when a tire went flat and they didn't have a spare."

Connor shook his head, disgust tightening his throat. "Fucking bastards. Were any of them from the Barton spread?"

"One of the deceased and two of the better-off ones, so they lucked out. They'll be returned in a day or two. I stopped here first, on my way to tell them."

Connor wanted to rush over and relay the good news himself, but knew he needed to keep his distance until he decided how to handle Tam Friday night if she showed up at The Barn. "They'll be glad to get back whatever they can."

"I hear Tamara might join us again this weekend." His friend sent him a shrewd look.

"Back off, Sheriff. We're friends, nothing more. I might show her a few more aspects, just to make sure she doesn't get into something she'll regret, but that'll be the extent of it," he insisted.

Grayson straightened, tipped his hat and said, "If you say so. I'll catch you later."

Watching him saunter back to his cruiser, Connor wondered why everyone was so sure there was more to his protection and friendship with Tam than he knew there was. *Idiots*, he thought with a touch of fondness. Just because Caden and Grayson appeared blissfully happy in their committed relationships didn't mean going down that road was for everyone. It sure wasn't his ideal path to follow. He was quite content remaining footloose and fancy-free.

TAMARA DIDN'T SEE or hear from Connor the rest of the week, which was a good thing. By the time she was leaving the clinic Friday afternoon, she'd worked herself into a state of frustrated indecision. She really wanted to go the club tonight, but every time she thought of expanding from voyeurism to exhibitionism, of someone other than Con seeing and touching her, uncertainty gripped her. The only thing she knew for certain was that sex was off the table.

Ever since she'd returned home for the summer following her sophomore year at college and she'd discovered she wanted much more from the neighboring rancher than friendship, she'd found no one she desired as much as Con. When he'd rebuffed her by taking off with an abruptness that hurt, she'd returned to college and wasted no time losing her virginity to the first guy who asked her out.

Pulling up in front of the house, she sat a moment, reflecting on that sunny afternoon ten years ago when the light brush of Con's lips over hers had affected her with a stab of heated awareness for the first time. She would never forget the stunning revelation of looking up at his rugged face and experiencing her first jolt of lust. The fact her close friend had been the one to stir up that pleasurable feeling had been jarring enough, but when he'd backed away as if burned, nothing could have prepared her for the hurt his first rejection caused.

"Aha! I won! That was a blast!" Laughing with exaltation from her first win, Tamara pulled Galahad to a halt in front of the stable, Con trotting up beside her. Breathing heavy from their race, she dismounted the same time as he did, turned and practically fell against him with glee. Clutching his arms, she felt the thick muscles bunch under her hands, the heat of his large body adding to the warmth of the summer afternoon. An odd shiver raced through her body as he looked down at her with that indulgent, crooked smile, his blue eyes lit with pleasure from under the lowered brim of his black Stetson.

"You cheated, sweetie." Tugging on her braid, he clasped her waist and brought her up against him for a hug. Just like he'd done thousands of times during the ten years of their friendship. "But I'll forgive you, like always."

His deep voice, so familiar and yet affecting her in a new, unfamiliar way, rumbled in her ear. "Did not," she returned as always, never tiring of their habitual banter.

He chuckled and her toes curled inside her boots. What was going on? *With a nudge under her chin, he lifted her face, and she knew what was coming, the quick touch of his mouth on hers, but was ill prepared for the rush of heat that light touch generated for the first time. Her lips tingled as soon as his ghosted across them, her nipples pebbled into uncomfortable tightness and the urge to press closer, open her mouth and plead for more was overwhelming. Startled, she jerked in his hold and looked up to see if he had the same response.*

"Shit." Con released her and swung about, leaping back into his saddle as if he couldn't stand to be there another second. "I've got to go, Tam. I'll see you around."

Watching him ride off, she knew she would never forget the first time he'd looked at her with something other than fondness. The surprise and regret in his eyes before his face had closed up cut her to the quick, and she knew her unguarded response had crossed a line he didn't care for.

Tamara sighed at the memory. She'd returned to college a few weeks later and other than the thrill she experienced from getting naked and doing the nasty without her dad or Connor threatening to shoot the guy, she hadn't seen what all the fuss was about. Luckily, there were a few men who had shared her bed since that night who were more experienced and considerate, but not even the pleasure of those encounters had given her the rush of her first light spanking a few days ago. Whether it was because she'd finally gotten Connor to put his hands on her in a non-platonic manner or because she might have a submissive streak she'd never known about remained to be seen. With any luck, she'd find the answer tonight, with or without his help.

Sliding out of her SUV, she spotted Amy riding up with Jason at her side, her stepmother's face pink from either the afternoon excursion or the look on her foreman's face when he glanced her way. Tamara hoped Amy wouldn't turn a blind eye to his interest. She wanted the woman who had welcomed her with open arms to find happiness again.

"Hey you two. What's up?" she greeted them as they strolled her way after tethering their mounts.

"I needed some fresh air and offered to accompany Jason on a ride to check the two heifers the sheriff returned this week. They're looking much better and we should be able to breed them soon."

Amy had been a veterinary assistant for a livestock vet when she'd met Tamara's dad and her experience had come in handy over the years. "That's good news." She looked at Jason. "Is Neil doing any better at fitting in and being careful?" Tamara had told him about the cigarette incident with their newest employee.

He nodded. "He is, but still has a problem with authority and punctuality. I'm giving him as much leeway as I can, this being his first ranching job."

"It's your call. You know the hands best, and what's needed from them. I appreciate your patience. I'm ready to get something to eat. You two want to join me?"

"Um." Amy fidgeted and cast a quick, uneasy glance toward Jason before saying, "We're on our way to get something at the diner. You're welcome…"

Tamara shook her head with a broad, approving smile. "No, thank you. I have plans in a little while. You two go on. Have fun."

"It's just dinner," Amy called out as Tamara veered toward the front porch.

"Okay, whatever you say," she replied with a quiet laugh as she bounded up the steps, happy for her widowed stepmother.

It would thrill her beyond measure to see the woman who had been more of a loving parent to her than her own mother happy again. Her father left the house to Amy and enough income to support herself, but monetary comfort couldn't make up for the loss of having someone special in your life. Tamara knew only too well how true that was. She'd missed Connor dreadfully during her self-imposed separation from him. Now that they'd reconnected and put that hurtful incident behind them, she couldn't bear to risk losing their connection again. Which was just one more reason why she had to force herself to get over her stronger feelings and the persistent ache for more than he wanted to give.

She arrived at The Barn just before nine o'clock with those thoughts still occupying her mind. Wearing the same black skirt she'd chosen for last week's visit and a white satin tank that tied at the shoulders, she hurried inside, refusing to second-guess her decision to return. If nothing else, that arousing light spanking Connor had delivered worked to increase her desire to continue exploring kinks she might enjoy.

As soon as she entered the empty foyer, Tamara realized she'd forgotten to ask Nan to meet her again. After hanging up her thigh-length sweater and stowing her shoes in a cubby, she reached for the door to the club with a nervous hand. But as soon as she stepped inside, a wave of excitement replaced her nervousness. This time she was ready for the sounds of people indulging in BDSM play and the comforting sense of friendship and affinity the members of this exclusive club portrayed. She started toward the bar where she spotted Avery and Sheriff Grayson, but Master Devin stepped into her path with an engaging smile of welcome.

"Tamara, it's good to see you again. I was just looking for someone to dance with. Interested?"

Caught off guard by his unexpected, quick interest, she hesitated, but only for a moment. Maybe it would be easier if she jumped into participating with someone she was now familiar with as opposed to sitting around fretting over who and what she wanted tonight. Master Devin's kindness and support last week was what she needed right now.

"Thank you. I'd like that." She took his hand, finger waving to Avery as they walked past the bar toward the small group of gyrating couples.

Not since her college days had Tamara let go on a dance floor, and as the music switched to a faster beat, a surge of adrenaline whipped through her. Smiling, she fell into the rhythm with Master Devin as easily as if they'd rehearsed their steps. He moved with a sexy assuredness she found attractive and fun, pulling her close, swinging her about and twirling her around. By the time the song ended, her heart was pounding from the fun exertion as she worked to catch her breath.

"You were great. Thank you," she panted. "I haven't done that in a long time." Before she could move away, he clasped her waist and drew her close as the next song began, this one a slow ballad with erotic lyrics that made her pulse skip.

"I'm good at slow dancing also," Devin returned with a confidence she'd noticed most of the Doms had in common. "One more. Unless there's someone else you'd rather spend time with."

There was, but since Connor wasn't of like mind, Tamara decided she couldn't do better or feel more comfortable than with Master Devin. "No, there's not."

"Good." Devin's dark blue eyes remained on Tamara's face as he drew her right arm behind her and held her wrist against her lower back, his hips swaying with hers as he pressed her against him. "Relax. Just like last week, nothing will happen between us you don't want and agree to. For instance, I would love to see your breasts." He lifted his free hand to the tie on her left shoulder, his fingers toying with the laces, his gaze patient but intent.

He was moving fast, she thought, but maybe that was a good thing. It gave her less time to think. And why not? It was just a boob, right? From what she'd witnessed last week and so far tonight, that small exposure was nothing. She found the slow swaying of their bodies pleasant, his secure hold of her arm behind her oddly titillating, both sensations bolstering her courage.

Since she wasn't sure she could get a word out around her dry throat, Tamara nodded in agreement. She should have known it wouldn't be that easy. These were not easy men in this place.

"I need the words, Tamara."

She swallowed and said, "Yes, okay."

"Thank you." With a quick tug, he released the bow and the left side of the silky top dropped far enough to expose her breast to the waft of open air and his heated gaze. "Nice." Brushing one finger over her nipple, the light graze drew the bud into a pucker. She sucked in a breath but despite the pleasure of that touch, she didn't experience the heat that one look from Con could produce. That disappointment only hardened her resolve to go even further.

Bending his head, Master Devin whispered in her ear, "I'd very much enjoy taking you upstairs and touching you even more."

Tamara nodded, determined to keep pushing forward. "I'd like that but reserve the right to back out if things get too…" She wasn't sure what she wanted to say. Too intense? Too uncomfortable? Too painful?

"You know the club safeword is red. Say it and I stop, no matter what I'm doing or how far we've taken the scene."

"That does help." She nodded. "Let's go before I chicken out."

He chuckled. "I like your honesty, girl."

CONNOR PULLED into the parking lot of The Barn and saw Tam's compact, white SUV. He had to take a moment to get himself under control before he went inside and risked laying into her again like the mistake he'd made before. She was a grown woman, free to come and go from his club as she pleased.

He didn't have to agree, or like it, but his brother and Grayson overruled his objections and left him no choice. Resigned to seeing her inside and to giving her another, more forceful lesson he prayed would deter her from continuing down this path and not jeopardize their relationship, he walked in with leaden steps.

Nothing, absolutely nothing could have prepared him for seeing Tam across the expanse of the playroom with one small, perfect breast exposed, her hand clutched by Master Devin's as the other Dom led her upstairs. His gut tightened, his throat closed and a myriad of emotions ranging from fury to lust filled him with a sense of impotency. He knew her, knew every nuance of her expressions. As he crossed the space with long, ground-eating strides, he could see the taut cast to her jaw and compressed mouth that portrayed determination, but the flash of uncertainty in her eyes as she took that first step up spoke volumes.

Before he could reach them, Caden stopped him with a grip of his arm. "Slow down and think, Connor."

"Get out of my way," he demanded, his need to step between Devin and Tamara growing stronger.

"Not until you settle down. We went through this already. You're being unfair. She wants this, so either tutor her yourself or leave her alone to continue with someone else."

Caden was right, he'd known that coming here tonight. But could he scene with her without losing or putting a wrench into their newly patched relationship? What choice did he have, did she leave him with? He'd been protecting her for years and wasn't about to stop now. For years before she'd moved away, Tam's eyes had held stars when she'd looked at him and he'd known she thought she wanted more from him than his friendship and their close bond. Since her return, he'd caught fewer glimpses of those stars, but they still lingered, and he didn't want to hurt her.

Being a guy and only human, he'd responded with both

surprise and lust to those hints of desire, but his Tam was made for a committed relationship that included home and hearth, and he wasn't. Once he showed her this lifestyle wasn't what she thought she wanted, he would gently let her know he wasn't the man for her and with any luck, they could return to their mutually satisfying friendship.

Taking a deep breath, he nodded at his brother, now under control and eager to get upstairs. "I'm good, Caden. But she's always been my responsibility, and that doesn't stop inside these walls."

Caden stepped back with a nod. "I think I'm beginning to see a lot more than you, little brother," he said to Connor's back as he watched him stop at the bar for a glass of ice before high-tailing it upstairs.

Chapter 7

Tamara chose the uncomfortable-looking, wood-slatted A frame when Master Devin gave her a choice of which apparatus she would like to try. The padded bench she had sampled last week had been comfortable, but she was counting on the discomfiture of this contraption to distract her from the public exposure and touch of a nice man again when she yearned for another.

"From the feedback I've heard, subs are enjoying our newest bondage equipment," he said as he backed her against the frame and lifted her right arm above her. "I'm glad you picked this. It's a lot different from the bench I strapped you on the last time. How does that feel?" He stepped back after securing her other arm and eyed her bound body with approval.

"It's okay." She didn't know how else to answer him regardless of his frown of disapproval at her short reply.

"You'll need to be a little more forthcoming, girl, if we're going to continue. Although," he drawled, turning his head as Connor approached them carrying a glass of ice, the possessive, determined glint in his eyes clearly visible without his hat. "It looks as if you might not need to answer to me much longer." He looked back at her with friendly curiosity. "Is there something between you and Master Connor I need to know?"

"No," she answered the same time as Con said, "Yes."

"Interesting," he murmured.

Devin's smile sent an uneasy quiver through Tamara, which turned into a full-body ripple of misgivings as Connor drew him away for a private chat. She couldn't make out their low voices, but the short discussion seemed to end on amicable terms as the two men returned to her, both looking satisfied.

"Tamara, with your agreement, Master Connor will continue with this scene while I relieve Master Greg from monitor duty. If, at the end of my hour commitment you wish to resume with me, I'll be happy to take back over." Cupping her chin, he lifted her face to meet his descending mouth. Whispering above her lips, he said, "I think it's best if you and Master Connor iron out your differences before you proceed with me, or anyone else."

He covered her mouth with his, kissing her long and deep, leaving Tamara in no doubt of his sincerity in wishing to return. By the time he released her, she didn't know if her trembling stemmed from that carnal kiss or the way Connor kept his unreadable gaze glued to them. Frustration mingled with a thread of excitement as she contemplated her decision. How could she refuse or move on when all she wanted the minute she saw Con was to get naked with him? A quick peek at him sealed her decision when she saw the banked heat in his cobalt eyes as they rested on her bare breast. The thrill of finally feeling his hands on her overrode the letdown of defeat.

With a jerky nod, she breathed one word. "Yes."

Master Devin inclined his head. "Connor."

"Thanks for understanding, Dev."

"Just don't make me regret it."

The steel edge in Master Devin's voice belied the friendly smile he walked away with. It was nice knowing she'd pleased someone enough he would look out for her. But as Connor stooped and tapped the inside of her right calf, a silent order to spread her foot over to the cuff attached at the bottom of the frame, she knew she didn't need or want anyone else. And wasn't that the crux of her constant, impossible dilemma?

Wrapping the soft, lined cuff around her ankle, he peered up at her, his eyes skimming her breast before settling on her face. "Remember, I'm Master Connor tonight and that I warned you this lifestyle wasn't for you. Other foot."

She shuffled her other foot over, saying, "I'll remember. And I plan to prove you wrong."

"Stubborn minx," he muttered under his breath as he checked the cuffs for tightness and then plucked an ice cube from the glass he'd set on the floor. "No talking unless you need to use one of the safewords," he instructed as he trailed the frigid cube up the inside of her right leg. "Red, I'll stop and end the scene and escort you out to your car." He slid under her skirt a few inches and then pushed to his feet, leaving a line of goosebumps down her leg and a burning desire for more. With his eyes on hers, Connor brought the ice to her neck and traced a path around her collarbone. "Yellow if you're unsure of something or need me to pause." She shivered as her body heat melted the ice into a cold trickle down her chest, his eyes warming her even more as they followed it. "Green if you're fine with me continuing. And, Tam?" His gaze whipped back to her face. Gripping her hair with his free hand, he tugged her head back. "I'll know if you lie."

The pull on Tamara's scalp coupled with Master Connor's stern tone and hot look sent her pulse soaring, the combined effect astonishing. "I've never lied to you," she reminded him, determined not to let him push her into retreating.

He smiled, the teasing grin all the girls fell for, the one she'd never been able to resist returning. "True, little one. Get ready."

That was his only warning before he circled her nipple with the ice, the frigid cold drawing the puckered tip into a tighter pinpoint. A low moan vibrated in her chest as she leaned her head back and closed her eyes. The hard frame failed to render an uncomfortable distraction from what she agreed to submit to; instead, the smooth wood and secure bonds provided security for her quaking body and offered only two choices for her to consider—stay or go. The minute she'd seen Connor coming toward her, the choice had been inevitable.

Tamara gasped, a small startled cry wrenched from her throat as Connor bared her other breast and tormented that nipple with another ice cube. Her torso broke out in goosebumps but the heat emanating from the nearness of his much bigger, broader body and occasional brush of his denim-clad legs against hers added enough warmth to keep her senses stirred up and vacillating between discomfort and arousal.

"Give me a color, Tam."

His deep voice resonated between them, drawing more heat, making her ache for more. "Green."

"Green what?" he reminded her with a pinch on her thigh.

"Master Connor." *Oh God*, why did that have to sound so right?

He brushed his fingers over the small throb and praised her. "Very good. Take a deep breath."

"Why?" she asked, keeping her eyes closed against the onslaught of rioting sensations he kept stirred up as she fought the growing need to beg for his hands on her.

"Because I'm going to do this."

With a quick shift of his hand under her skirt, he slid the ice inside her panties, withdrew his fingers and cupped between her legs to move the cube around. Tamara screeched in shock, her eyes flying open as she gasped and writhed in the restraints. To her astonishment, the inability to free herself combined with the numbing effect of the ice heated her blood into a torrential molten rush through her veins. Or maybe it was the warmth of Connor's palm through the thin silk of her panties that was responsible for her off-the-charts response. His low chuckle in her ear didn't help.

"You should have obeyed my directive without questioning me. Let's try again. Deep breath."

This time she didn't hesitate, just sucked in as much air as possible and looked down. Watching his hand move under her skirt, he pulled what was left of the ice out of the front of her panties and around to the back, sliding his hot hand and the icy cube over her bare buttocks. "Connor," she groaned, thrusting her pelvis forward in a silent plea for more of his touch, for something to ease the throbbing ache in her pussy.

Pulling his wet hand from her panties, he smacked her thigh. "*Ow*! What was that for?" she demanded, glaring at him despite how that sudden burn ramped up her arousal.

"Speaking and not addressing me properly. Color."

She narrowed her eyes, rising to the challenge etched on his face. "Green, *Master* Connor."

THIS WAS NOT GOING WELL, Connor thought as he looked down at Tam's flushed, determined face, her gray eyes glazed with frustration and lust. His plan to show her this lifestyle wasn't for her with a demonstration of sensation play had backfired on him with her response to the ice. Convincing Devin of his desire to protect Tam from herself had been easy compared to trying to deter her from the course she'd set herself on. He didn't know whether she was pushing this to get back at him in some way or because she possessed an honest interest in embracing sexual submissiveness. Neither was acceptable for his peace of mind, and he refused to relinquish her to someone else.

"Good enough," he returned, trying not to smile at her disgruntled frown. "But I'll caution you about your tone. You can push me all you want outside these walls, in fact, I like it when you do. But in here it's my way, as I command, or not at all."

"Unless I go back to Master Devin," she taunted.

Every muscle in his body cramped up from the image that popped into his head of his friend fucking Tam, another unacceptable possibility. "Then I'd best make sure you don't want to do that."

Following a light caress over the top of her chest, he slid his hand down and cupped one breast. Small and firm, the plump softness was a perfect fit for his wide palm. The delicate pink nipple beckoned for attention, a lure he found himself powerless to resist. Dipping his head, he licked the turgid tip and felt each nub under his tongue before opening his mouth to take in as much of her soft flesh as possible. Her taste was intoxicating, her breathy moans stimulating and the arch of her body pressing her breast closer irresistible. He cupped her other breast, kneading the cushiony mound as he suckled harder on the treat filling his mouth while laving the nipple over and over. Tam's cries turned to mewls as she twisted her torso, thrusting her breasts ever closer to his face. With lips and teeth, he drew up on her nipple, elongating the tip before releasing it with a plop and then straightening to gauge her reaction.

Her breathing came in pants that jiggled her breasts as she yanked on the restraints. "Had enough?" he asked with forced politeness, praying she said yes. Instead, she gave a wild, negative shake of her head, sending her cloud of midnight silky hair flying around her shoulders. Left with no choice but to give in for now, he cupped her nape, arching her head back so he could rest his brow on hers as he reached under her skirt. Palming the damp heat between her legs, he wondered how much of the wetness came from the melted ice and how much had dripped from her pussy. Is that why he'd put it there, so he wouldn't know if the ice play turned her on?

Connor groaned at his stupidity. "Every time I heard you

were back visiting, I hoped you would stay, or at least talk to me." He pressed up against her crotch. "Now that you have, I find myself in the strange position of thinking you were better off in Boise, away from me."

"How can you say that?" she asked, their mingled breath filling the small space between their faces, the sounds of BDSM play resonating around the loft going unheard.

"How can you push me into something I don't want to do?" he returned without thinking.

Shit. Connor realized his mistake as Tam stiffened and answered that unintentionally hurtful question with one word. "Red."

TAMARA WENT COLD, remorse and despair replacing the euphoria that had been building since Connor had taken her over so fast it made her head spin. "Let me go," she demanded, her voice emerging as shaky as her emotions.

He pulled back, his hands reaching to free her wrists, his tone laced with regret as he said, "Tam, I'm…"

Shaking her head, she lowered her arms and pulled up her top. "It's Tamara. I keep telling you I'm no longer a child and don't need nicknames, or apologies for being honest with me." As soon as the cuffs fell away from her ankles, she stepped out of his reach and tried retying her top.

With an impatient brush of his fingers, he shoved hers aside and made short work of securing each side and then snatching her hand before she could avoid his reach again. "We can discuss this later, away from here and all the distractions. Come on, I'll walk you out." He surprised her by halting at the bottom of the stairs, gazing down at her with a worried expression and reluctant resignation as he offered, "Unless you'd rather stay and wait for Master Devin."

Because he did offer, and Tamara could see how much it pained him to do so, she declined. How could she stomach another man's hands on her when she could still feel Connor's calloused touch and her body ached with a need she feared only he could assuage? "No, thanks. I'm ready to go."

TAMARA RETURNED from a long vigorous ride the next afternoon to find the horse stalls hadn't been cleaned or strewn with fresh hay, a chore that should have been done hours earlier. Lady, her new mare, remained corralled instead of being turned out to pasture to graze, which added to her irritation of waking tired this morning after tossing and turning in frustration all night. She didn't need this added grief, she thought, dismounting and tethering Galahad. Maybe she would be in a better mood if she'd used her vibrator last night, but she hadn't wanted a fake phallus, no matter how much pleasure she'd always gotten from it in the past. Now that she'd felt Con's hands on her, she wanted him more than ever. Damn it.

She reached up and stroked her steed's sleek neck, murmuring, "Who needs the jerk, right boy? You're the only guy I need, aren't you?"

Galahad tossed his head and then butted her shoulder. She laughed and unsaddled him, glad to see Lady trotting over for attention without being coaxed. The little mare had been shy when she'd first brought her home but was slowly warming up to both Tamara and Galahad. The loud rev of a running motor drew her attention as she opened the gate to turn both horses loose in the field. Seeing Neil rolling to a stop by the cattle barn, apparently just now showing up for work, stirred up Tamara's annoyance as she remembered the stalls that still needed cleaning.

She strode across the yard, working to rein in her temper

until she made sure he didn't have a good reason for missing half a day's work when he hadn't completed his three-month probationary period, as was standard for new hires.

"Where have you been?" she asked with a slight edge to her voice.

"Sorry." Neil sent her a sly grin. "Partied too hard last night. Don't worry, I'll get my chores done."

"That's not the point, Neil. I can't put my horses up until the stalls are cleaned, and Lady hasn't been out to graze all morning."

"Well, why didn't you turn her loose?"

Narrowing her eyes, she questioned, "Excuse me? I believe you are assigned to the horse stable, and I have other chores, not to mention…" Tamara halted as Jason and Amy emerged from the barn, Jason's pleased expression mirroring her stepmother's until he looked at Neil and frowned. *Does everyone have to look so friggin' happy together?* Shrugging off the unfair observation, she kept quiet and let her foreman take over.

"It's about time. Early afternoon is not a little late." The reprimand didn't sit well with Neil if the angry glint in his eyes meant anything.

"Hey, I said I'd be late, not how late. I'll get to work," he added hastily when Jason's frown turned to a glower. He stomped off toward the stable, attitude written in every angry step.

"Are you sure we should keep him?" Tamara didn't speak lightly of letting someone go, but Neil needed a wake-up call, at the very least.

Jason huffed in frustration. "No, but with the threat of rustlers still active, we can't be a man short while I look for a replacement. But I can start the ball rolling if you want."

Tamara shook her head with a sigh, seeing the question about her sour mood in Amy's eyes. "It's your call. I guess we can give him more time to settle down. Maybe not a lot more though."

"That was my thought." Jason squeezed Amy's shoulder before stepping back. "I'll check on him in a little while. Did you find the fencing I thought needed replacing?"

"Yes, and I agree. Go ahead and give me the list of what you need. I'm headed in to order supplies now."

"I'll give you a hand," Amy said, falling in line with her as she pivoted toward the house. "I thought your ride would put you in a better mood."

"Am I that obvious?"

Amy grinned, pulling open the front door. "Only to me as I know you so well. Connor?"

"That man is driving me nuts," she bemoaned, leading the way into the kitchen where she poured them each a glass of iced tea.

"Sweetheart, men were born to drive us women crazy. Life would be boring though if they didn't."

Amy's endearment reminded Tamara of how Con had switched from calling her sweetie to little one after her disgruntled protest. He was thoughtful like that, which had made it so easy to fall in love with him right after a bad case of lust had replaced adolescent worship as soon as she was mature enough to know what those stirrings were whenever he was near. "I'd go for boring if he'd quit thinking of me as the kid he'd befriended twenty years ago."

Amy hugged her with a light laugh. "Oh, Tamara, can't you see? His little head has already acknowledged you're a very desirable, grown woman. Their big heads are always much slower to respond to the obvious."

"Really?" Tamara teased her in return. "How long have you been fighting your attraction to Jason?"

"That's different." Amy sniffed with a toss of her head. "I've loved a wonderful man already and was lucky enough to have his love in return. That's harder to work through than what you and Connor are struggling with."

"I know, and I'm sorry." Tamara squeezed Amy's hand. "I miss Dad too, but at least you now seem open to more, and I'm glad."

"I'm taking it slow and he's patient. I just hope his patience lasts until I'm ready."

They left the kitchen together and padded down the hall toward the office as Tamara said, "Yeah, well my patience ran out, and I was all set to have a little fun by moving on. But, oh, no, *he* had to interfere."

"And how did he go about that?" Amy asked, settling behind her desk as Tamara strolled over to the larger, ornate mahogany desk that was her father's and now hers.

She flipped her stepmother a self-deprecating smile as she sat down. "He strode up to me and the man I'd hooked up with and looked at me with those bluer than blue eyes."

Amy raised a slim brow and her lips twitched. "The jerk. No wonder you were doomed. So, now what?"

"Now I go back and try again and hope it'll be easier to tell him no."

When Amy left for the afternoon to attend a cattle auction with Jason, Tamara went back to brooding over Connor's reluctance to move beyond friendship and her inability to think about anyone but him, to want no one but him. By the time she had finished eating a solitary dinner, she couldn't get up any enthusiasm for changing out of her comfortable loose jeans and old college sweatshirt and into the short black skirt, let alone to return to The Barn.

After taking a batch of carrots out to Galahad and Lady, she curled up on the sofa in front of the television until she heard Amy return. Not wanting to answer questions about her change of mind, she turned in early, praying she slept better than she had last night.

"You have company," Amy said the following afternoon, her

announcement startling Tamara and she jerked, banging her head inside the oven she was scrubbing out.

Scooting back, she sat on her heels and looked up at her stepmother with a frown. "I'm not expecting anyone. Who is it?"

"Us." Nan, Sydney and Avery breezed into the kitchen, the three of them wearing identical smiles that reeked of a conspiracy.

"Hi. What's up?" Tamara asked, suspicion tightening her abdomen as she glanced at Amy and saw she was in on whatever was going on.

"This is an intervention." Nan grabbed her arm and pulled her to her feet. "No need to change, it's just us girls, pizza and wine. Emphasis on wine. Let's go."

"Where to?" Tamara couldn't help but be pleased over the prospect of not spending another long evening brooding as she followed her friends to the front door.

"To our house," Sydney answered. "Caden is at Connor's playing poker with a bunch of other guys, so we have the place to ourselves."

"And I, for one, am more than ready for some girl time that involves lots of wine. I swear, Grayson gets more and more protective instead of less now that my ex and his partner are going to jail."

"What's he worried about?" Tamara asked Avery as she waved goodbye to Amy and slid into the backseat of Sydney's car with her.

"Who knows? He says he doesn't trust them, but I think he just likes being bossy." Avery sighed, but the small smile curving her mouth hinted she wasn't all that put out by the sheriff's demands.

"They all like being bossy. Haven't either of you figured that out yet?" Nan swiveled to face Tamara and Avery from the front passenger seat as Sydney drove toward the Dunbar Ranch.

"Which is precisely why I intend to stay footloose and fancy free, playing the field, committing to no one."

"I predict our friend falls before the end of the year," Sydney announced.

Tamara laughed. "No way. I've known her a long time. Nan loves her independence."

"Yup, almost as much as I love giving it up for a few hours of sexual submission. Nothing beats that. Speaking of which. That's why we're hauling your butt out of the house tonight. We've decided you've pouted enough over that man. That is why you didn't show last night, isn't it?"

"He's driving me crazy," Tamara admitted as they pulled up in front of Caden's sprawling ranch home, the front porch lit up to guide their way inside.

Nan eyed her with a shrewd look. "Would it help if I told you he left early last night after rebuffing several subs obvious interest?"

"He did?" That tidbit perked Tamara up until she forced herself not to read too much into it. "I don't care. He can play with whoever he wants."

"That blatant lie is why we're going to take your mind off the pigheaded jerk with lots of junk food and alcohol. And then you will forget all about him and think about Master Devin when I give you graphic details of some of his scenes, especially the ones with me. Did you know he and Master Greg are into sharing?"

"Huh?" Tamara's face warmed. "I can't even bring myself to choose one man other than Con and you want me to consider two at the same time? No way, no how."

The three of them burst into hysterics at Tamara's stunned utterance as they gathered around the pizza strewn kitchen table. "Hey, don't knock it until you try it." Sydney flicked Avery a sly grin. "I *loved* the scene Caden set up with Grayson."

Avery scowled and gave her a mock growl. "I told you to never bring that up."

"Sorry, couldn't resist." Sydney's green eyes filled with amusement as she passed a bite of pizza to each of the collies who had followed them inside. "Don't tell Caden," she warned them.

"I will if you bring up that scene again," Avery threatened even though she had slipped the dogs some herself.

Tamara's mood lightened considerably listening to her friends' banter. It wasn't long before she was laughing with them, stuffing her face and on her fourth glass of wine. They moved into the den after finishing off the food, each carrying a bottle and a glass. Settling on the floor, they sprawled out, giggled like schoolgirls and talked trash on men.

"So, how did Master Connor get you away from Master Devin the other night?" Nan wanted to know.

Tamara was tipsy enough to tell her the truth. "He walked up to us and looked at me with those gorgeous eyes."

"The rat bastard."

Nan's feigned disgust drew another round of hysterical laughter before she turned thoughtful and tapped her lips with one finger, humming, "*Mmmm.*"

"Uh, oh. She has that gleam in her eyes," Sydney said.

"I'm thinking Tamara needs to do something that will get Master Connor to see her in a different light. And I have just the thing. You need to ditch the black skirt for something I would wear to the club."

"Oh, that's good." Avery nodded her head in agreement as Tamara's throat went dry thinking about some of the outfits she'd seen in Nan's closet.

"Shopping trip!" the three of them cried in unison.

Ever skeptical, Tamara shook her head. "And if he doesn't fall for the bait?"

"Then someone else will, no question about it."

Nan's positivity rubbed off on her enough to get her agreement, but she refused to hope for success. That would only add to her heartbreak if she failed again. By the time ten o'clock rolled around, they decided it wouldn't be smart to let Nan drive Tamara home on her way back to Willow Springs since she was as drunk as the rest of them. Sydney texted Caden for assistance and much to Tamara's dismay, Connor arrived with his brother and her entire body grew hot at the way he zeroed in on her with that enigmatic blue gaze.

CONNOR TOOK one look at Tam's glassy eyes and his heart rolled over. "You are so not supposed to be here, crashing my fun," she muttered.

"Well, I am. If not me, who?" She looked as young, as innocent and as drunk as when he'd picked her up from her first bonfire teen party after she'd called for a ride. That was back then, when she listened to him and hadn't hesitated to obey when he instructed her to contact him if she'd been drinking after he had learned where she planned to go.

"I'll drive Tam home." Ignoring Tam's emphatic, negative head shake that made her lose her balance, his brother's derisive snort and Grayson's taunting grin, Connor strode into the den and hauled her to her feet, his eyes sweeping the floor strewn with empty wine bottles and candy bar wrappers. "You girls went through a stash, didn't you?"

"Yeah." Avery sighed and leaned on Grayson as she yawned. "It was fun."

"Just wait until morning." The sheriff tugged on her hair as he steered her toward the front door. "Goodnight everyone."

Connor grabbed Tam's hand, noticing she didn't argue or fight his hold, and followed them. "I'll be out after therapy tomorrow, Caden. Dan, do you have Nan?"

"Yeah, I'll either get her home or she can crash at my place if I don't feel like driving into town by the time we reach my turnoff. Come on, Legs. Up you go."

"Have I ever told you I like your nicknames?" Nan murmured as she batted her eyes up at the lawyer. "You are so frickin' hot."

"Good to know," he returned with a fond look.

They were quite the group, Connor mused as he lifted Tam into his truck and pulled the seatbelt around her, grateful for her silence. She'd been on his mind all day, the same as she had ever since he'd heard she had returned to stay, and he still didn't know what to do about the tightrope they were both walking regarding their relationship. He wanted to stay on the end where it was safe, but she kept insisting on pushing the boundaries into uncharted, dangerous to his peace of mind and libido territory.

Shutting the door, he strolled around to the driver's side and settled behind the wheel, glancing over to see she'd already fallen asleep. She was so much easier to deal with inebriated, he mused. Shaking his head, he followed Grayson and Dan down the drive toward the highway, resisting the temptation to draw Tam against his side. It was bad enough he hadn't been able to drum up any interest in playing with a willing sub again last night and couldn't forget how her nipple puckered under his stroking tongue, how soft her breast was or how her breathy moans and arching body stirred him. He refused to compound his dilemma by feeling her soft body pressed against him and her warm breath fanning his neck in the dark, quiet of his truck.

Connor pulled in front of Tam's house ten minutes later, her soft snoring sounding loud in the compact space, his mouth twitching to break into a smile as he came around to lift her out. She stirred as he set her on her feet at the door.

Leaning into him, she whispered in an achingly young voice, "Connor, I missed you."

He sighed and rested his brow on hers, replying as Amy swung the door open. "I missed you too, Tam. That's why I'm trying so hard not to make another mistake."

"Well, this looks familiar," Amy drawled. "I'll take her from here, Connor. Thank you."

"No problem. That's what I'm here for. Goodnight."

Well, heck. Tamara watched with bleary eyes as Con strode back to his truck, his words ringing in her head. *That's why I'm trying so hard not to make another mistake.* How could she fault him for that?

Chapter 8

"Jeremy, I've asked you to stop calling." Tamara wished she hadn't answered his call but ignoring them the last few days hadn't worked. She didn't need the added aggravation of her ex's refusal to accept the end of their relationship on top of everything else she'd had to deal with this week. Between Neil's continued tardiness and half-assed efforts on his chores and a close call with losing more cattle to the rustlers, she had her hands full. At least the diligence of the rest of her hands and those of the neighboring ranches in keeping watch for the thieves had paid off. The last she heard, the authorities were tracking down license plates and descriptions and everyone was hoping for good news.

"There's no reason we can't stay friends," Jeremy insisted. "In fact, I was thinking about making a trip to see you, give you a chance to show me what's so appealing about running a ranch."

"No, that would not be a good idea. I'm way too busy and there's a lot going on." His presence was the last thing she needed right now.

"Like what? Wouldn't it help to share your burden?"

She snorted. "What can you do about rustlers and a difficult employee?" Not to mention a stubborn cowboy she couldn't quit thinking about getting naked with.

"Take you away from all that?" he returned with a hopeful note in his voice.

The door to her therapy room opened and Tamara looked up from behind the desk, her heart jumping as Connor walked in. She thought of the leather corset dress she'd let Nan talk her into buying yesterday, pictured his face when he saw her in it and went hot all over, her pussy going uncomfortably damp. "I'm working and have to go," she told Jeremy before clicking the phone shut and smiling. "Hi. Any luck?" He'd canceled his Monday appointment to help follow the lead on the rustlers.

"Some, not enough." Tossing his hat on a hook, he ran a frustrated hand through his shoulder-length, brown hair. "The authorities in the next county found the truck our guys spotted and they're pulling prints, so we'll see if anything comes from them. At least this time they got away empty-handed."

"There's that. Sit down and I'll check your shoulder."

Sinking onto the mat, Connor gave her an assessing look. "How was your head Monday morning?"

Other than his text to cancel his appointment, they hadn't spoken since he'd dropped her off Sunday night. "As you might expect. You've been overdoing, you're tight."

"I'm fine," he insisted.

"And you call me stubborn. I would suggest giving it a rest, maybe applying heat to loosen you up, but you won't listen, so I won't bother. Let's skip the pulleys and I'll go over some new stretches you can work on." Tamara turned and took two steps toward the file cabinet when he stopped her with his next question.

"Are you returning to the club Friday night?"

"Honestly, Con," she replied without looking back at him, "I haven't decided." Which was true. Every time she imagined herself wearing the dress she'd bought, at her friend's insistence yesterday, to the club in front of all those people, she wanted to call Nan and back out.

"Here." She handed him the papers showing the stretches. "Try these along with some heat. I'd planned for this to be your last appointment, but maybe you should let me check your progress one more time next Monday."

Pushing to his feet, he pinned her with those blue eyes. She couldn't read his expression or figure what he was thinking, but his look alone made her uneasy. "I'll behave if you will, Tam." Stepping around her, he grabbed his hat and opened the door. "Later, little one."

Two days later, Friday morning started with Jason telling her on her way out he'd fired Neil. "I'm sorry, but I caught him smoking, this time inside the barn, and that's a risk I refuse to take no matter how much he swore it wouldn't happen again after you reprimanded him the first time," he said, opening the car door for her.

"I agree. It's difficult putting someone out of work, but we gave him several chances to straighten up. But, now we're short-handed." Tamara slid behind the wheel and Jason shut the door then leaned in the window.

"Yes, but I'll get someone hired this weekend. At least the rustling is likely to stop now that two of them have been caught."

The two men in custody were identified by their fingerprints taken from previous arrests. Deputies picked them up yesterday and everyone was hoping they would roll on the others. At least five men were involved in the ring that they knew of for sure.

"That was the best news of the week. Have a good day, Jason."

Tamara's mood stayed upbeat until she returned home that evening, dressed and rode out to The Barn with Nan. She started second-guessing herself before they pulled into the parking lot and her nerves kicked into high gear as soon as they entered the foyer and the faint strains of music and BDSM play filtered through the door to the clubroom.

"I still can't believe I let you talk me into this." Tamara hung up her long sweater in the foyer closet and tugged on the indecently short hem of the body molding bustier corset dress. The tight, elastic fit cupped under her breasts while just inching over far enough from the sides to cover her nipples. The stretchy leather hugged her hips, upper thighs and butt, leaving her back bare except for the narrow halter tie, the crisscrossed red laces down the front and cutout sides exposing just as much skin.

"You look fantastic, and you won't be alone," Nan told her for about the fifth time since picking her up. "The guys love fetish dress night. I still think you should have given Amy a peek at you."

"She's wonderful, open-minded and supportive, but still my stepmother. It would have been way too embarrassing. Are you sure I can leave my shoes on?" The three-inch black heels not only gave her height, but made her bare legs appear much longer.

"Fuck me shoes fall inside the dress code. Trust me on that one. Connor is going to take one look at you and swallow his tongue." Nan smiled at the prospect.

"Or he'll give me that spanking he's threatened me with," Tamara returned dryly. "This thong is driving me nuts."

Nan's quick glance was both sympathetic and devious. "I've kept myself waxed for years and I still struggle with the distracting sensations of soft silk brushing over that exposed, sensitive area. Don't you just love it?"

"Let's say if what I'm feeling doesn't keep my mind off Con, nothing will." As soon as she'd slipped the silk thong on after shaving and felt the soft brush against her bare labia, Tamara had almost come undone. Tiny prickles of pleasure kept spiraling up her pussy every time she moved, warming and distracting her in a delicious, naughty way that made her wonder what other sensations a man's touch might magnify.

"Oh ye of little faith. I say he'll snatch you up tonight before someone else does. And if he doesn't, I'm sure Master Devin will be more than happy to pick up where you two left off last week." Wearing nothing but a leather corset that provided a shelf for her full breasts and a thong, Nan appeared at ease in her skimpy attire.

Tamara's clammy palms almost slid off the slick dress as she ran them down her sides, praying she wouldn't have to settle for someone else tonight. Taking a deep breath, she nodded for Nan to open the door before she could change her mind. Entering the club, her gaze swept the room and found Con lounging in a small seating area off to the right. Her pulse skyrocketed as she took in his relaxed pose. With one booted foot crossed over his opposite knee emphasizing the snugness of his jeans, his Stetson pulled low on his brow and an open leather vest exposing his bare chest and arms stretched along the back of the sofa, he exuded sex and a confidence she'd give anything to possess a fraction of.

The married couple she'd met once sat across from him, Sue Ellen lying in a boneless heap across Master Brett's lap, her husband running a casual hand across her puffy, bright crimson buttocks as he conversed with Connor. Tamara knew how much trouble she was in when she found herself envying the woman, more so when Con looked up and nailed her in place with one searing glance.

"Whoa, I don't think you have to worry about him rebuffing you tonight, girlfriend. Have fun." Nan took off as Connor came to his feet, Caden having just joined the trio.

"HERE WE GO AGAIN," Caden muttered, stepping in front of Connor.

"What's that supposed to mean?" Connor wasn't in the mood for his brother's interference. He couldn't believe Tamara showed up here dressed like that. She may as well hang a sign around her neck that said, 'Fuck Me'. The hypocrisy of his disgruntlement wasn't lost on him, but he chose to ignore that.

"It means stop and think, again. I swear, you two will drive everyone nuts if you keep this shit up. Take my advice. Give her what she wants tonight, both of you get it out of your system because you want her as much as she wants you, even though you refuse to admit it. Then let it go, just like you've done a hundred times before." Caden lectured him with exasperation underscoring each word.

"She's not just another sub." And wasn't that the problem? he admitted. Because Tam wasn't just another in a long line of women. Taking the chance she could either threaten his desired bachelorhood or end up so hurt their relationship wouldn't survive scared the hell out of him.

"Tonight, allow her to be one. Either that or leave her alone." Caden stomped off, having made his point.

With slow measured steps, Connor crossed to where Tam still stood by the doors, never taking his eyes off her flushed face. The more he looked at her in that dress, with her breasts all but spilling out and her toned legs going on forever, the more he knew she wouldn't be with anyone but him tonight. He couldn't think about tomorrow, or cave to the fear that sliced through him whenever he thought of losing their special connection. She was responsible for the untenable position she had put him in, but he vowed he wouldn't let her run away again come tomorrow when she realized he'd been right, that this lifestyle wasn't for her.

He stood before her, still towering over her even though she wore heels. Nudging his hat back with one thumb, he gazed down into gray eyes that revealed a longing he was hard pressed to continue ignoring. Placing his fists on his hips, he cocked his head and asked, "You're not going to give up on this idea, are you?"

"Why should I?" she returned, her soft, breathy voice stirring his cock and sealing his doom for the night. Connor prayed what he was about to introduce her to wouldn't spell catastrophe for what remained of their friendship.

"Just remember, this is what you've insisted you want." Holding out his hand, he knew she wouldn't turn him down, not after braving coming here dressed like that. That alone drilled into Connor just how serious she was about continuing to explore this lifestyle.

He tugged her toward the sofa he vacated, noticing Brett now cuddling Sue Ellen on his lap as he conversed with Greg and Devin who stood by their sofa. Perfect.

"What are you planning, Con?"

The uncertainty in Tam's voice would have been a good sign he might not have to take this too far if he hadn't also caught the thread of excitement she couldn't hide. "That's Master Con, first and last warning, and whatever I want, little one. That's part of what it means to submit to me." Taking a seat across from the other couple, he saw her give the four of them a quick glance before looking back at him.

"What's the other part?"

"Me giving you not only what you want but discovering what you need and seeing to that as well." He patted his thighs and bit back a smile when she tried to take a step back. Too bad he still held her hand and stopped her with a quick yank that caught her off balance and tumbled her over his lap.

Flipping her hair out of the way, she turned her face up to him, the flash of arousal in her eyes at odds with the surprised quaver in her voice as she stuttered, "You… you're going to spank me? Why? What'd I do?"

"Nothing," he replied, keeping his tone bland as he rested his hand on her leather-covered ass and felt her buttocks clench in response.

"Then… I don't understand."

Confusion was good. Keeping her unbalanced and on edge would, with luck, end this before it went too far. "I enjoy tormenting my subs, dishing out long spankings and am especially fond of ass play." He inched his hand down to her smooth thigh, her muscles tensing under his palm as he glided under the tight stretch of her skirt. Pushing up the hem, he cupped the underside of one plump globe.

Tamara flicked a look toward their audience, who were still conversing in soft tones but looking their way, the men with indulgent smiles, Sue Ellen with sympathy. A flare of heat lightened her eyes before she jerked her head down and wiggled her butt. "Fine," she croaked.

Connor had been hoping for more resistance, her quick acceptance boding ill for a fast end to this scene. Resigned to continuing, he pushed the skirt all the way up, baring her fucking perfect ass, the narrow string of her thong bisecting her buttocks a sexy draw for the eyes. Smoothing his hand over her cheeks, he took his time enjoying the soft mounds, squeezing and plumping her flesh until she relaxed with a sigh.

"Very good, Tam." He punctuated his praise with a light tap that didn't even jiggle her buttock. Continuing in that vein, he snapped his cupped fingers across both cheeks, setting up a steady rhythm of teasing flicks, entertaining himself and the others. There was nothing more fun than ass play, but one peek at her glistening slit told him it was time to up the ante.

Pressing his left hand on one thigh to steady her, he delivered a sharp smack that pulled a startled gasp. "Problem?"

"No, just wasn't ready," she mumbled.

"You remember the safewords, right?" he asked with the next swat.

"Yes." She nodded, swinging her hair.

"Good. Keep quiet now unless you need to use one."

Connor spanked her again, and again, increasing the strength by slow increments while maintaining a regular, smooth tempo that built up a heated redness over her quivering backside. Her gasps changed to low moans as he smacked her harder, the moans turning to whimpers that accompanied the shift of her hips under his hand.

"Be still or I'll ask Master Devin and Master Greg to hold you," he warned. The quick way she stopped moving drew amused chuckles from the men.

Connor drew out the spanking, slowing and then speeding up, softening his blows before adding a bite of sharp pain with harder slaps. He kept a practiced, careful eye on Tam's face and body, making sure he didn't push her too far but enough to give her a good example of pain play. From the continued dampness glistening between her legs, he figured he didn't need to fret over going too far. Which meant it was time to move on to phase two. A lust-induced thrill stirred his senses as he smoothed his hand over her burning flesh and ran through his options. If she insisted on pushing him into taking her further, he would follow Caden's advice and get this unasked-for craving for a taste of her out of his system.

"I'm proud of you, Tam," he told her, adhering to honesty as he helped her sit up. She winced as her naked butt landed on his denim-covered thighs but the glaze of arousal in her pewter eyes spoke volumes, confirming his inability to turn her off from this pursuit.

Resigned to his fate for the evening, he nudged her face up with two fingers under her chin and made sure she was steady enough and aware enough before hauling her upstairs. "Do you need a moment, little one?"

The little minx shifted her ass against the press of his erection and shook her head. "No, Sir. Now what?"

There was no mistaking the eagerness in her voice that

matched the excited expectation etched on her face. "Shit. I swear you'll be the death of me someday. Come on."

TAMARA LOCKED her knees as she stood and realized how wobbly her legs were. With her buttocks throbbing with heat, her pussy aching with a neediness she'd never felt before, she took a deep breath and followed Master Connor as he drew her toward the back stairs. Thank goodness he'd tugged down her skirt even though she admitted to getting an illicit thrill from the exhibitionism part of her first over-the-knee spanking, a spanking those few taps he'd given her at the clinic hadn't prepared her for. Never in her wildest imaginings could she have envisioned the sheer eroticism of a bare-butt spanking, not to mention how arousing she'd found it to be. Now, with Connor's urgency coming through loud and clear giving her hope this would all work in favor of advancing their relationship, she trotted up the stairs eager for whatever he planned to do next. As she'd suspected before tonight, if it was Connor's hands, mouth and eyes on her, she was game for just about anything.

"Do you need help with getting out of that dress?" he asked as they reached a spanking bench.

The music drifted upstairs and blended with the murmured voices and soft, tormented cries resonating around the dim loft. The bench appeared to be the only piece of equipment unoccupied, but that was fine by her.

"No, at least I don't think so."

"Then strip while I get a few things."

Tamara watched him saunter over to a wall cabinet as she shimmied out of the stretchy leather, the brush of cooler air drawing her already puckered nipples into beaded pinpoints as her breasts bounced free of the tight confines. Master Connor returned carrying several objects, the sexy bristles covering his bearded jawline failing to hide the tense tic in his cheek. She knew the second his eyes landed on her denuded labia and hoped that hot gaze meant he was losing his battle to resist her.

"Why is it," he drawled, tossing his hat and stroking one finger over a nipple, "you can continue to surprise me after all these years?"

"I'm good at it?" Her teasing grin slipped as he circled her nipple and then plucked at the tender nub until she leaned into his hand with a groan. With his riveted, undivided attention focused solely on her, she found it easy to block out the rest of the activity going on around them.

"Yeah, you are. Do you know what these are?" He held up a pair of wicked looking silver clamps, each attached to a four-inch long, one-inch wide metal tube.

Unsure, Tamara shook her head, unable to talk around the lump lodged in her throat. Having knowledge of things such as nipple clamps was one thing; experiencing them firsthand was another. The spanking had started light and enjoyable and ended much harder, yet she found all of it titillating. But the intimacy of lying across his knees and feeling the flat of his hand connecting with her vulnerable backside made that an awesome, desirable experience. Just looking at the metal clamps attached to the strange canister produced a shiver of alarm; not that she feared he'd hurt her, but that she would fail this test.

"Give me a color, Tam."

The command, delivered in his usual warm, friendly tone held an underlying note of steely insistence. Tamara chose the safest answer. "Yellow, Sir."

"Good girl. It would have displeased me if you avoided the truth." Connor dropped the two oval objects attached by a short cord he held in his other hand onto the bench and then opened the clamp on one of the nipple toys. "These are wireless vibrators. They're perfectly safe but can get intense." He clipped the clamp on her nipple, the slight pinch more arousing than painful;

that was until he tightened it and she yelped. "Breathe through the pain, it'll settle in a minute. Use yellow again if they become too much for you to handle."

Tamara sucked in a breath, both to bear down against the discomfort as he attached the other clamp and to bolster her determination to show him she could handle whatever he dished out. Master Connor's constant, sharp vigilance in watching her with those assessing eyes was as effective at soothing her nerves and warming her heart as when he gave her a similar look as just Connor, her friend.

A small smile played around his lips as he picked up the other objects off the bench, boosted her up and nudged her shoulders for her to lie back. The clamps and attached tubes tugged on her already pulsing nipples, but when he pressed the buttons on the bottom of the tubes and tiny vibrations encircled her tips, her entire body erupted into a fiery inferno of need.

"Connor!" she cried out without thinking, her hands automatically rising to cover her breasts. A stinging slap on her thigh snagged her breath, the burn working against her ability to hold out as long as possible.

"That's Master to you and keep quiet unless you need to use a color." The rebuke lost some of its effect since his grin had spread into a smile wide enough to reveal a flash of straight, white teeth. He reached up and removed her hands, placing them down at her sides before securing each wrist to a strap he wrapped around each thigh. "How does that feel?" he asked, running a finger inside the cuffs, testing the tightness.

Tamara tugged, the yank against her legs feeling strange and arousing at the same time. "It's fine," she answered as he pulled off her heels and brought her feet up to lay flat on the end of the bench.

Connor nodded, lifting his eyes to her face as he ran his hands down the insides of her thighs from bent knees to crotch.

"Good." She held her breath as he looked down and used his thumbs to spread her glistening folds.

Embarrassment warred with a suffusion of pleasure. Tamara tried closing her legs, but a pinch to her labia halted her effort. As he reached for the egg-shaped objects, she finally recognized the dual bullet vibrators from her search for a personal toy. Her entire body quaked as he dipped between her buttocks and pressed the lubed egg against her anus.

"Relax and bear down," he instructed, lifting his gaze to her face once again as he gave a delicate push against her back orifice.

"Easy for you to say," she muttered.

"Do you wish to say red?"

A pang clutched her abdomen at the look of hopeful expectation on his face, but she refused to let that hurt cut into her resolve to see this night through. After all, it might be the only chance she would get to experience this side of him. "No way."

"Stubborn to the end." With a harder push, Connor embedded the small vibrator inside her butt, his other hand never stilling in rubbing the inside of her leg with soothing caresses. He dipped two fingers inside her gaping pussy, his teasing smile returning to loosen his tight lips. "You're so wet, this one will slide in with no problem." With a quick thrust, he proved his point, snuggling the larger of the two toys deep inside her vagina.

Tamara squirmed, trying to adjust to the foreign invasions that shifted along her inner muscles as she moved. Spasms of pleasure tickled her insides, surprising her with the strange but arousing sensations erupting in her rectum.

"That was the easy part." He palmed the remote and flicked the switch, setting up a series of soft pulses that would have sent her flying off the bench if she hadn't been bound.

"Oh my God," Tamara groaned, slamming her eyes shut against the rapid rise of arousal and knowing glint in Con's eyes.

The touch of his calloused fingertips along the sensitive skin of her vulva drew a shuddering sigh and she couldn't keep from lifting against his hand.

"Like that, do you?" he purred in a silky voice. "How about this?" Dipping his thumb inside her pussy, he stroked each side of her clit, tracing the swollen nub with a touch too light to give her the push she both craved and feared.

Biting her lip, Tamara kept her eyes closed despite the desire to catch what Master Connor was thinking on his face as he touched her. The myriad of sensations rolling through her body from her tortured nipples, down to her throbbing pussy and anus and the continued calming brush of his hand along her thigh threw her into a tailspin of rioting emotions. While she hadn't been celibate the last few years as she pined for Con, nothing could have prepared her for the firestorm of pleasure his touch ignited. Not even the arousal her most vivid, wildest fantasies had unleashed had come close.

Applying a steady pressure against her clit, he rasped in a strained voice that forced her eyes open, "Give me a color, Tam."

"Green." Who needed to think when he'd reduced her to a mass of pulsating flesh and hot neediness?

"Shall I see how many times I can make you come?" He pressed harder against the inflamed piece of aching flesh and stopped rubbing her thigh long enough to up the vibrations inside her swollen orifices.

An orgasm hovered, the small contractions preceding the big bang rippling along both vibrators, but she shook her head, bit her lip and tightened her muscles against giving in to the pleasure. This *had* to go on longer. She needed to wring as much from his attention, from his touch as possible because who knew what mood he would be in tomorrow? "No, I… I can't," she begged, her sweat-slick body straining against the bonds and the escalating pleasure.

God, he looked sexy standing between her splayed legs, his

hands working on and in her body, his thick, muscled chest and arms taut with his own struggle, his blue eyes smoldering with a flame of lust he couldn't keep from her. If that was all she could get from him tonight, then she wanted to draw it out for as long as possible.

"I say you can." Leaning over her damp, quivering body, he continued to toy with her clit and play around the entrance of her pussy while stroking her thigh as he licked over each turgid, throbbing nipple. His voice turned hard and frustration, either with her or himself flashed in his eyes as he looked up and breathed against her trembling mouth, "Now, little one."

Instead of kissing her, like she yearned for, he delivered a delicious nip to her lower lip, the prick of pain matching the stabbing needles of agony engulfing her nipples as he leaned back, plucked the clamps off without warning and began milking her clit. The sudden, painful cessation of stimulating vibrations and easing of compression shot her off like a rocket, her astonished cry resonating in the surrounding space. Mind-numbing pleasure spiraled through her body, her hips bucking against his marauding fingers as her vaginal and anal walls clutched at the toys still vibrating against them.

Tamara was still catching her breath, still quaking from the small aftershocks rippling through her when Master Connor removed the vibrators and went to one knee, burying his face between her trembling thighs.

"Oh, shit," she whispered, her fingers itching to sink into his tawny hair and pull his head away before he drove her past the point of sanity.

She could feel his low laugh against her saturated flesh resonating all the way up her core and had no choice but to tighten her thighs against his head as he speared her depths with tongue and fingers at the same time. Her back arched, thrusting her reddened, stiff nipples upward as she pressed her soaked pussy closer to his invading, decadent mouth. A soft, wet stroke lashed over her clit. The press of two fingers against tender nerve endings drew a gush. Teeth nibbled and a tongue soothed. Rough beard bristles tickled and scraped against the tender skin of her inner thighs. Fingers scissored, stretching and teasing before thrusting deep enough to bump her womb. Heat that had just begun to cool returned hotter. Tight vaginal grips that had eased back clutched even harder than before. Contractions built with each finger and tongue stroke until her entire lower body convulsed in a series of climaxes that stripped her of cognizant thought and awareness, thrusting her into a vortex of blinding lights and flooding sensation.

Chapter 9

Connor lifted his head from feasting on Tam's saturated flesh. Her taste coated his tongue and lips and he could still feel her soft thighs pressed against his face, the tight grip of her climaxes soaking his invading fingers and stroking tongue. Coming to his feet, he ran his hands down her shaking legs, wondering how the hell this hadn't gone as he'd planned, as he'd needed it to. He had intended to make her wait, to torment her by withholding her climaxes in the hopes the frustration would force her to admit his sexual proclivities weren't for her. Instead, he'd found himself powerless to resist the need reflected on her face and in the supplicant gyrations and wetness of her body, her slick heat and soft cries too tempting to ignore.

His cock pressed with painful intensity against his zipper, leaving him desperate for relief. He'd drawn out her pleasure and withheld his too long. One touch would set him off, a touch he knew he could get from any number of willing subs. But looking down at Tam's flushed face, her chest heaving as she struggled to steady her breathing and regain her senses, he knew there was no way he would do that to her. He may not like how her mere presence had pushed him into topping her tonight or her continued insistence on exploring what his club offered, but that was his problem. There was no choice but to ease his tormented state with her. God help him.

Lowering her legs, Connor flicked a knob on the side of the bench, raising her head halfway up. He couldn't fuck her – thrusting inside her snug body would cross a line he knew neither of them would succeed in crossing back over to where they were, where he needed their relationship to be. That left him one other option.

Connor ran the pads of his fingers down her damp face as he carefully lowered his zipper, freeing his hard as steel erection. "Are you with me yet, little one?"

Tam blinked her eyes, trying to focus on his face, her lax body revealing the toll multiple orgasms had taken on her muscles. "Getting there," she returned in a drowsy whisper, the small smile of contentment playing around her mouth causing a tightness in his chest.

He slid his fingers to her cushiony lips as he gripped his cock and stroked over the smooth, damp crown with his thumb. "*Oh*," she breathed softly, her small tongue darting out to lick his fingers as the sated glaze cleared from her eyes.

A shiver racked his body, and he cursed the strong effect that sexy gesture produced. "Tell me," Connor uttered, pulling his right leg out of his jeans and straddling the narrow bench at her shoulders, "are you as good at giving as you are at receiving?"

"I'm as good at *trying*, at least when it comes to this." She leaned forward and swiped her tongue over his seeping slit. "Let me try, Master Con. Please."

With a jerky nod, he let her lead as he worked to get himself under control. The Dom side of him preferred to take charge by holding her head, rendering her helpless as he used her mouth. But the long-time friend and protector side still ruled with Tam and held him back.

"Go ahead." He brushed his cockhead over her lips,

spreading the pearly dribbles as she licked every inch of the mushroom cap before dipping under the rim to tease that sensitive area. His muscles went taut as he fought to hold back the pleasure.

Tightening his hand around the base, he hissed in a breath as she found his sweet spot. She closed her lips over him, bending her head forward to take several inches into her warm, wet mouth. He saw her jerk on her still bound hands and knew from the low groan that vibrated down his shaft she wanted to touch him, but that would not do. He was too far gone to hold back against the feel of both her mouth and hands.

Soft lips clung as she drew back with a hard suction that sent tingles racing up his spine, her tongue a constant swirl of stroking, tasting motion that drew ripples of hot pleasure licking up his shaft. Connor struggled to breathe and hold on, but as Tam shifted her legs behind him to coast one slender, bare foot across his buttocks, he yanked back and pumped his seed onto her quivering breasts. The room spun as he closed his eyes, threw his head back and released a low, guttural moan of body-clenching pleasure, his grip tightening to the point of discomfort.

Connor opened his eyes as his brain started to function again and the first thing he saw was Tam's adoring, gray-eyed gaze. The second was her semen-splattered chest, white streaks marking the soft skin as she drew shuddering breaths that shook her breasts. The urge to lean down and kiss those swollen, slightly curved lips prompted him to lower his head. It was the brush of her breath against his mouth that jarred him into full awareness of where he was, what he'd done and with whom. *Jesus*. Shaken by the strength of the climax she'd pulled from him and the jeopardy he feared this night had put their relationship in, he jumped back and moved off her. With a hard thrust, he shoved his leg back into his jeans and pulled them up. Freeing her hands, he helped her up, wincing as she fell against him in a boneless heap, her sigh tickling his neck, the pinpoints of her nipples drilling into his bare chest.

"What the fuck am I going to do with you now, little one?" he muttered into her ear, wrapping his arms around her and holding her close to help steady both her and himself.

Tam held on for a moment before leaning back, holding onto his forearms. "I don't know. Only you can answer that as I don't think you really want my suggestion."

"No," he sighed, taking her hand, "I don't." After tossing the toys in a bin to be cleaned later, he snatched up her dress, shoes and his hat and tugged her toward the stairs with no other thought in mind than to step away from her for some much-needed contemplation time.

Luck was on his side for a change when he spotted Nan and Avery soaking in the hot tub as soon as he reached the lower floor. Perfect. "Come on. You can join your friends and relax while I get a drink." *And question my sanity in agreeing to scene with you.* Opening the glass slider, they stepped onto the deck and out into the refreshing cool night air. Tossing her clothing on the bench, he slapped his hat back on, saying, "Ladies. Would you make room for Tam, please?"

"Sure." Nan scooted over, unabashed in her nudity while Avery, sitting opposite her, shifted lower on the seat, as if the swirling, bubbly water would hide her full, bobbing breasts. Still new to the lifestyle, she appeared comfortable with her nudity when Master Grayson was by her side but turned shy whenever he left her alone without offering her the comfort of covering herself.

"Thank you." Turning, he lifted Tam and swung her over, looking away from the hurt and confusion on her face as he grabbed a bottle of water from the outdoor cooler. Opening it, he handed it to her. "Drink all of that so you don't get dehydrated. Get dressed and come find me when you're ready and I'll take you home." He stalked back inside before he could do something stupid, like strip and join her.

"THAT MAN IS BLINDER THAN A BAT," Nan muttered. "He's so far gone over you he can't see it. We should get him back out here by giving him a show he won't be able to ignore." With a wicked smile, she reached up and toyed with one pouty nipple until it pebbled under her finger.

Tamara shook her head, disappointment and denial crushing her hopes. She knew better than her friend Con was not 'gone over her', at least, not the way Tamara wanted him to be. Her body ached in the most delicious way and the hot, swirling water helped ease her tense muscles. But nothing could lessen her despair over ever getting past the brick wall of protective friend Con had erected between them. She couldn't dispel the vision of his face hovering above hers, his lips so close to her mouth she felt the wisp of his breath. Her heart clutched as she recalled the startled horror in his eyes before he'd pulled back, as if the intimacy of sharing a possessive, man and woman kiss as opposed to the friendly peck they usually shared was something he couldn't fathom or bring himself to do. God, that had hurt. "You're wrong, Nan. Didn't you notice how fast he ran from me now that he's finished our scene? He's not interested in more."

"Besides," Avery put in, shying away from Nan's nipple play. "Master Grayson would tan my butt if I masturbated without his permission."

"That's why I intend to stay free of a monogamous relationship. When not in a scene, I can do as I please." Nan cupped both breasts and rasped her rigid nipples with her thumbs, a sigh of pleasure parting her lips as the buds puckered even tighter. "I still say he's fighting how much he wants you, Tamara."

"I just want to go home." Tamara refused to believe that or

look into the playroom. She didn't want to know what Con was doing, or how determined he was to put what just happened between them out of his mind. For her, there would be no forgetting the taste of him, the feel of his hands and mouth, the exalted high he had driven her to. Her nipples still throbbed from the tight clamps and soft vibrations and her pussy and rectum still spasmed with remembered pleasure.

Dropping her hands, Nan sat up straight, her drowsy look turning fierce. "Well, you're not running inside to him to drive you. I'll take you and his order be damned. Like you said, you're not in a committed relationship."

Avery frowned. "Uh, is that wise? From what I've learned, none of these guys will hesitate to punish you for disobeying a direct order."

Wise or not, Tamara liked Nan's idea better than seeking out Con. She was done running after that man, finished with hoping for something he would never be agreeable to. "Thanks, but Connor's fought putting his hands on me since I returned. He won't mind. And I don't want to argue with him on the way out."

Nan pointed to a stone path that wound alongside of the barn. "Dry off, get dressed and follow that around front to the parking lot. I'll meet you at my car with our jackets." She looked at Avery with a challenge. "If asked, I plan to tell Master Connor Tamara is still out here with you."

Avery winced but nodded. "Okay, I'll stay until you two have left. What are friends for, right?"

"Thanks, both of you." Tamara waited until Nan dressed and slipped inside before forcing herself to leave the comfort of the heated, bubbly water. Goosebumps popped out all over her body as she snatched a large towel off the bench and hurried to get dry. Her skimpy dress wouldn't be enough cover against the much cooler night air, which was even more of an incentive to move fast in getting out of here.

"I hope you don't get into trouble with the sheriff," she said, stepping to the side of the barn so no one could see her from inside as she struggled back into the stretchy, leather dress.

"If I do, it won't be the first time. Besides, it's for a good cause. I hope you and Master Connor work things out," Avery replied with soft concern.

"Oh, we'll manage to stay friends, and with any luck, someday I'll get over this ridiculous, one-sided infatuation and we can stay close." The way she was feeling now, with her heart aching as much as her well-used body, Tamara doubted her own words. But hope springs eternal and all that, she thought as she slipped on her shoes. "Thanks again, Avery." With a wave, she dashed around the side of the building, shivering from the cold, her lips still aching for Connor's aggressive assault, her body longing for the rough possession of his cock.

"Here." Nan thrust her long sweater at her as soon as she came out the front doors, just seconds after Tamara reached her car. "Connor did ask about you but believed me when I said you were still out back. Let's go."

Sliding into the passenger seat, Tamara turned toward her friend as Nan drove down the narrow, tree-lined road leading back to the highway. "I'm sorry. You didn't have to leave early on my account."

Waving a hand between them, Nan hurried to reassure her. "I'm fine, Tamara. I already enjoyed Master Greg's attention, so it's not like I'm missing out. Besides, I talked you into exploring the club. I'm not about to ditch you when a pig-headed Dom walks away from you."

Tamara felt the need to defend Con. "He made sure I was steady… you know, afterwards."

"Well, duh. I never said he wasn't a *good* Dom, just a pig-headed one." Pulling in front of the Barton ranch house fifteen minutes later, she put the car in park and swiveled toward Tamara with an earnest suggestion. "Don't give up on him, Tamara. Of all the guys I've known, Connor and Dan have always been the most foot-loose and fancy-free, always insisting monogamy and commitment weren't for them. But look how fast Caden and Grayson fell."

Tamara frowned. "Connor has been in a few long-term relationships, from what I've heard."

"Sure, and I think Dan has also, but they didn't last because they weren't the right person. You are, for Connor, he's just too stubborn to see it. Besides, you two have a bond I, and everyone else envies. That's a hell of a lot more to go on than most relationships start with."

"That's just it, Nan. He doesn't want to jeopardize our special connection, and I'm tired of going where I'm not welcome." Reaching for the door handle, she swung it open and got out before Nan talked her into hoping for something she knew wouldn't happen.

Nan looked toward the porch, her eyes turning sharp as she asked, "Who's that?"

Tamara whirled so fast her long sweater swung open, revealing her risqué attire to Jeremy's astonished gaze as he stood at the top of the steps, waiting for her.

Surprised disbelief turned to irritation as Tamara jerked her cover closed. "Jeremy? What the heck are you doing here?"

"What the heck are you wearing, and where have you been dressed like that?" he returned in an angry tone she'd never heard him use before as he stomped down the steps.

"Should I stay, Tamara?" Concern laced Nan's voice.

"What?" Looking back at her friend, she dipped her head inside the car, whispering, "He's my ex and no threat, I promise, other than to annoy me right out of feeling guilty for breaking up with him. Go on, I'll be fine."

"If you're sure. Call me later."

"I will, I promise." Tamara waited until Nan drove away before facing Jeremy again, not caring for his belligerent stance of arms folded across his chest, his brown eyes glaring at her with accusation. "You have no business showing up here, unexpected and uninvited," she snapped, weary of his refusal to accept the end of their engagement. "I'm sorry you came all this way for nothing, but I'm not inviting you in, Jeremy, and have nothing further to discuss with you."

He stepped toward her, his sneer changing to a look of contriteness she recognized. "I'm sorry, baby. Seeing you looking so sexy threw me for a loop. I didn't even know you owned a dress like that."

"I didn't until this past week, and that doesn't matter." She stepped around him as he made to reach for her. "Jeremy, please." She sighed, wishing he didn't keep forcing her to hurt him. "I do not love you and am not getting back with you or returning to Boise. I don't know how to make it any clearer. Please go." Looking around, she spotted the back end of what she assumed was a rental sticking out on the side of the house, relieved he had transportation and wouldn't have to wait around for a ride.

"We'll talk tomorrow," he insisted, his mouth tightening. "I saw a motel as I came through that small town on my way here. I'll get a room there and call you in the morning. You can show me around this place, as a friend, nothing more. I swear."

She didn't believe him and besides, she already had a male friend who had her tied up in knots, she didn't need another. "No," she returned sharply. Trotting up the stairs, she fished out her keys wishing Amy were still up to open the door. "Don't call, don't return here. Goodbye, for the last time, Jeremy." She didn't look back again as she let herself inside the lighted foyer, closing and locking the door behind her. Leaning against it, she waited until she heard his car start up and the tires crunching on the gravel drive before she pushed away with a sigh of relief.

Padding into the kitchen, she spotted Amy's note propped up on the table. *With Jason. I'll see you in the morning.* "Well, at least one of us is happy tonight," Tamara muttered, pivoting toward the freezer. Grabbing a carton of ice cream, she settled at the table with spoon in hand and a heavy heart until she heard the approach of another vehicle. "Welcome to Grand Central Station," she grumbled, swearing if that was Jeremy returning, she would threaten him with a restraining order, guilt or no guilt.

The Barn, thirty minutes earlier

Connor stayed outdoors after Grayson ushered Avery back inside. He could tell by the sheriff's look he wasn't happy with her subterfuge, but they both knew the blame belonged to Tam and Nan. Tam was the one who had disobeyed his instructions to come find him so he could take her home after she'd recuperated in the hot tub. He'd wanted that quiet, alone time with her to assure himself she was okay after that intense scene. Of the three, Nan knew the rules and the Doms best and she shouldn't have aided and abetted her friend in disobeying them and then lied to him about it. It would be up to him to decide the experienced sub's punishment, but not now, not tonight.

Leaning his forearms on the rail, his gaze shifted from the darkened trees up to the nighttime, star-studded sky. Tam's hair was as inky black as the endless expanse above him and he used to love watching the way her long tresses would fly out behind her as she galloped across the fields, her body swaying in tune with her horse as her high-pitched laughter of sheer delight reached him on the wind. She'd been twelve when she had attempted her first jump over the fence separating their properties and he'd never forget the way his heart lodged in his throat as she tumbled off going over. He'd made a mad dash across the field, his hands trembling with worry only to find her laughing on the ground, looking up at him red-faced with exhilaration.

Just like that afternoon, tonight he didn't know whether to

throttle her for worrying him by taking off without giving him the chance to ensure they were still on good footing or hold her close until he could get his conflicting emotions sorted out.

"I see you're brooding again."

Connor replied to Caden without turning around. "Go away."

"That's original. You obviously weren't happy with Tamara since you pawned her off after your scene, and yet you're still pouting now that she's gone instead of going after her like any self-respecting Dom would, and should do. Why don't you give it up and go claim your girl?" Caden drawled with a hint of irritation. Moving up to the rail, his brother cocked his head as he peered down at Connor who refused to straighten from his contemplative position.

"She's not my girl the same way Sydney is yours."

Caden snorted rudely. "You're so fucking pig-headed."

Connor straightened and glared at him. "Damn it, Caden. She's white picket fences and PTA meetings and I'm… this." Frustrated, he thrust out an arm toward the activities going on behind the sliding glass doors.

Remaining calm, Caden asked, "Why can't she, and you be both?"

He flicked him a derisive look before turning back to the rail and bracing his hands on it. "Yeah, right. Can you see me tied down to one woman?"

"If she's the right woman, then yes. But since you can't, consider this and then answer that question yourself. It took me a while, but I managed to put two and two together. Last fall, your mood swings mimicked those of a woman going through menopause and started right after you ended things with Annie."

"Yeah, so? She cheated on me, and I never made a secret of why we split," he replied, wondering where Caden was going by dredging up old history.

"My memory must be better than yours, because I recall you

were already showing less interest in her a few weeks before that, right about the time rumors of Tamara Barton's engagement reached town."

An annoying clutch gripped Connor's abdomen. "What's your point, Caden?"

Caden laughed and slapped him on the back. "Think about it, brother of mine. I think you've known for a while she's the only one for you."

Connor looked at Caden's retreating back with a puzzled frown. *What the hell was he talking about?* But the longer he stood there, gazing out at nothing as he thought about what had gone through his head when he'd heard Tam was to get married, the more he realized how obtuse he'd been. His morose mood swings had started about that time, his discontent with playing here at the club had also begun soon after hearing about her engagement. And wouldn't you know it? He'd been in a better mood and frame of mind ever since he'd learned she had returned home for good after ending her wedding plans. "Son of a bitch," he swore.

When he couldn't drum up any enthusiasm for seeking another sub and picturing Tam with another Dom pierced his gut with a stab of painful fury, he lost the final battle to hold himself in check. He'd been right to back away when she first showed signs of wanting more than friendship from him. She'd been too young ten years ago, barely twenty and in college, and he'd just started exploring his interest in the BDSM lifestyle. But he'd been wrong to push her away five years ago, a complete ass for taking out his fear of change and of losing their special connection on her in a way that sent her fleeing.

Pushing away from the rail, he stalked around to the parking lot as a familiar thrill shot through his body, one he'd been denying for weeks, ever since experiencing it upon seeing her in his club the first time. His heart thudded and his cock stirred as he imagined making Tam his in every way.

Connor pulled into the Barton's drive in time to catch the taillights of a departing vehicle. Assuming it was one of the ranch hands taking off for the night, he hopped out and strode up to the front porch, stopping only when Tam flung open the front door wearing a cute scowl that changed to a comical, wide-eyed look of surprise. Stifling the urge to grin, he pasted on his best Dom face and stalked toward her with slow measured steps, never pausing until she backed up and he entered the house. Closing the door behind him with a loud snick, he stalked toward her, a tingling buzz of lustful expectation he hadn't felt in way too long dancing down his spine.

"What are you doing here?" she asked with suspicion and a flare of excitement shining in her eyes.

"For starters, to confess I've been an idiot."

One slim brow winged up as she retreated another step. "I won't argue with that."

Connor let the lust that had been simmering under the surface for weeks free to take him where he now knew, without a doubt, he wanted to go. "You want change between us, and I've always tried to give you what you want, right?"

TAMARA'S PULSE spiked as she continued to back away from Con, Master Con if she wasn't mistaken by the look on his face and in those cobalt eyes. Her pounding heart tumbled, just like the first time she'd gazed into those enigmatic eyes. Several years later, that tumble had included a flutter in her abdomen, the same tickle now tightening her stomach. Soon after, she'd been old enough to respond with a damp clutch between her legs to go along with the tumble and flutter, the same reaction she experienced the minute she opened the door and saw him coming toward her with a look of intent purpose.

He hadn't put on a jacket or even a shirt, and she found

herself hard-pressed not to rush forward and lean against all those rippling muscles just so she could see if his heartbeat matched the chaotic rhythm of hers. Regardless of the surge of heated awareness gushing through her veins and a giddy sense of relief and happiness warming her chest, she refused to make this easy for him.

"What changed your mind?" she asked as he backed her against the wall inside the kitchen and tossed his hat onto a chair. The gleam in his eyes tripped her pulse and made her question whether she should just go with this sudden change of heart or continue to question his about-face.

"Let's just say big brother Caden pointed something out to me." Connor spotted Amy's note and nodded his head as if satisfied with what he read before shifting his glance toward the melting ice cream. A rueful twist curled his mouth as he cut his gaze back to her. "Double chocolate chip. You must be really upset with me. Let's see if I can remedy that."

Before Tamara could grasp his intent, Connor braced his hands on the wall behind her, leaned down and gave her what she'd been craving for years. The kiss was as forceful, demanding and mind boggling as she imagined it would be. He didn't start soft, didn't coax his way inside her mouth and didn't tease her into returning the kiss. His lips moved with rough possession over hers, his tongue shoving past her trembling gasp to forage inside her mouth and stroke, lick and explore. To take.

Tamara clung to him, and what he was finally offering. He shattered her will to resist and made her desire to surrender to him with the first glimpse of hot need in his eyes. The first touch of his mouth on hers as a man kissed a woman, using the control of a Dom kissing his sub, sealed her fate. A low moan slid up her throat as he inched closer, the brush of his big body and bunched muscles emitting enough heat to make her sweat. His warm breath fanned her neck as he released her clinging lips and nipped the delicate skin near her shoulder.

"Connor?" She heard the confused stutter in her voice as loudly as her body was suddenly clamoring for release.

"You've always been my girl, Tam." He slid his right hand off the wall to fist a wad of her hair, using his tight hold to tug her head back. The yank on her scalp caused her sheath to spasm and her breath to stall. Dipping his head, he whispered in a rough growl that curled her toes and dampened her pussy, "Now, Tamara, let's see if you can handle being my sub."

Chapter 10

Connor was finally looking at her as a woman, calling her Tamara instead of Tam for the first time since she'd been ten years old, and offering her a chance to be his in every way. The pang clutching her chest upon hearing her full name from his lips took her by surprise, but she would examine the reason for that later, much later. Right now, she had better things to do, like relieve the itch in her fingers to reach up and tug on the crisp, brown curls spread across his thick pectorals.

"I can handle whatever you dish out, *Master* Con," she breathed against his corded neck before sinking her teeth into the tanned skin and then soothing the bite with a slow lick. She knew better than to laugh at his shudder and low curse.

"Minx." Keeping his hand in her hair, he shifted his free hand down to the hem of her short dress and rucked up the stretchy leather until he had it bunched around her waist. With one hard yank, he ripped off the thong and tossed the torn scrap on the floor.

The sudden bare exposure drew a shiver, the touch of those calloused fingers on the delicate flesh of her denuded labia brought her to her toes. The aching need only he could conjure up and assuage returned tenfold and she thrust her hips toward his hand with an urgent plea. "Please."

Connor dipped his head with a low laugh, biting down on one nipple through the dress. "Such a pretty word falling from such a pretty mouth."

"You're teasing me, and that's just plain mean," Tamara complained, gasping as he skimmed those wicked fingers up her slit. She thrust her hips forward again only to receive a reprimanding, stinging swat on that tender area. Her shriek echoed in the kitchen, her full-body shudder drawing another rumble of amusement from her friend turned tormenter. "Crap!"

"Lesson one." Connor grabbed her bottom lip between his teeth and tugged. "When it comes to sex, it'll be my way, including when and how you will get your pleasure. Remember, you asked for this."

"A long time ago," Tamara reminded him, her throbbing lip matching the thrumming going on between her legs, both egged on by the burn encompassing her puffy folds.

"Want me to make up for lost time?" He dipped two fingers inside her, brushed over her swollen clit and then pressed against that small spot that triggered a gush of cream with every touch.

"Yes, God, yes." Digging her nails into his chest, she relished his indrawn breath and rapid heartbeat. Sliding over to his nipples, she tugged on the small brown tips and it was his turn to moan as the nubs pebbled under her touch.

"You're playing with fire, little one," he warned with another deep thrust, his other hand tightening in her hair.

Tamara smiled against his chest. "I thought I was playing with you."

"Same thing. Reach into my front pocket and pull out the condom."

She didn't want to take even one hand off his hot flesh, but retrieving the protection meant she was one step closer to having her dream of Connor surging inside her come true. Her fingers brushed the side of his thick erection through the pocket as she pinched the small packet and lifted it out. He hissed a breath but never slowed his strokes inside her quivering pussy. Heat enveloped her entire body, drawing beads of perspiration down her back and quickening her breathing. Using her teeth, she ripped open the packet and then looked up into his dark face, waiting for his instructions.

"Good girl. Never assume you know what I want you to do." Releasing her hair, he proved how talented he was as he continued to pummel her pussy while releasing his cock into his other hand.

Tamara struggled to control both her breathing and her need to let go. She wanted this to last even though her achy body was screaming for release.

"Cover me," he rasped, putting pressure against her pulsing clit.

Shaking from the small contractions rippling around his pumping fingers, she made short work of rolling the latex down his straining shaft until she reached his fisted hand. "Now?" she begged, brushing her fingers over his, jutting her pelvis forward to add a silent plea.

"Now." Connor pulled his fingers from her pussy, grabbed both of her hands and pinned them against the wall as he kicked her feet apart with a large booted foot.

Eager, more than ready, Tamara welcomed his first penetrating thrust with a soft cry, the rough stroke over the inflamed tissues carrying her right to the edge of a climax. She gasped as the second plunge knocked her over that precipice, leaving her no choice but to hurl headlong into ecstasy. Within seconds of being pinned against the wall by his plunging cock, she found herself spiraling out of control with sweeping pleasure so intense it left her stunned. Shaken, she gasped and raised her right leg, curving around his battering hips, tightening her thigh to hold him closer.

More, more, more. Tamara didn't realize she'd verbalized the chanting thought until Con swore and ground his mouth down on hers as he rammed into her over and over. Another orgasm claimed her body even before the first had abated, forcing mewling cries past her constricted throat to fill his mouth.

Connor groaned, his chest heaving, his cock quickening inside her. She rippled around him, her muscles clutching at his girth and pulling his seed up from his sac. He wrenched his mouth from hers as he spewed inside the condom, and she wished she could feel the hot jets of his cum filling her vagina as a third round of pleasure rocked her with its endless pulses and fiery heat.

JEREMY HINES STOPPED at the roadside bar he had passed on his way to surprise Tamara at her ranch, still reeling from seeing her in that slutty dress and then watching that tall cowboy stroll inside her house as if he owned the place, and her. The man hadn't even flinched from being out in the cool night air wearing nothing but an open vest and jeans, the fucking moron. What the hell had gotten into the woman he loved, the quiet, almost reserved fiancée who had shared his bed? She sure as hell had never teased him by wearing something so risqué, so cock-hardening revealing. He grabbed an empty stool at the end of the bar, sitting next to a young guy wearing a disgruntled frown that matched Jeremy's mood.

The place was teeming with cowboy roughnecks, annoying, twangy country tunes blaring as a line of patrons stomped their booted feet to the beat. He shook his head, wondering what the hell Tamara found so appealing about living out in the boonies on a smelly ranch with the nearest town no bigger than one of Boise's suburbs.

"Whiskey, double," he ordered from the bartender as the older man approached. He hadn't booked a return flight yet because he didn't know how long it would take him to convince her to come back with him. From his reception, he doubted now his success in changing her mind. "Women," he muttered, wishing he could get over her as easily as she appeared to have gotten over him. Just thinking about that spurred his anger and made him wonder if she'd ever intended to marry him.

"I hear you, man," the guy next to him growled in a slurred voice. "Bitches, all of them, especially if they happen to be your boss."

"Working for a ball-breaker, are you?" Jeremy asked in sympathy as he accepted his drink from the bartender.

The guy snorted. "Not anymore. I had a good thing going until the Barton bitch decided to come home to ruin things."

Jeremy almost choked on his drink and had to take another sip to force the first down. *What were the odds*? "Did… did you say Barton?"

Squinting blurry eyes, the guy groused, "Yeah, why?"

"I know her, and I'm as unhappy with her as you." Jeremy kicked back another, longer swallow, the liquor searing his throat as much as Tamara's betrayal burned in his gut. The more he thought about her ire when she'd seen him, her clothing, and that cocky bastard she welcomed inside, the hotter his anger grew. "Too bad you're not still on that fucking ranch," he said without thinking. "I'd pay to show her she doesn't belong out there."

Eyes sharpening, the younger guy held out his hand. "I'm Neil. Let's talk options."

CONNOR REMAINED FIRED up on all cylinders as he pulled out of Tamara's clutching body, still feeling the way her tight spasms rippled up and down his cock and how her abundant cream had made it easy for him to plow into her without stopping until he'd exploded. Her leg fell back down, and he missed that possessive clasp that spoke volumes. He could just make out her glazed eyes in the dim lighting, the damp flush covering her face and the outline of her pert nipples. Looking further down, past the rucked-up dress, he gazed a moment at her glistening, puffy labia, aching to delve between those slick folds again.

"Are you in your old bedroom?" he asked gruffly as he lowered his shoulders and hoisted her face down over his right.

Her startled gasp followed with a giggle that warmed his heart. Palming one buttock, he strode down the hall as she replied with a breathless gasp, "Yes. Are you staying?"

The hope in her voice tugged at his conscience. He'd been blind for way too long. Tossing her onto the double bed covered in a handmade quilt of bright colors, he stated, "All night, so I hope you can get by tomorrow on little sleep. Get out of that thing."

As soon as they'd both stripped down to nothing but bare skin, Connor joined Tamara on the bed, flipped her over and yanked her hips up. Her hands fisted in the covers as she pushed up onto her elbows and turned her head far enough for him to see the flare of excitement in her pewter eyes and the teasing grin kicking up the corners of her lips. "It's taken me forever to get you here and now *you're* in a hurry?"

"I may be slow, but once I'm where I want to be, I don't believe in wasting time." He coasted his hands across her soft buttocks. "I owe you a spanking for leaving the club without my permission, or even the courtesy of telling me, but you're still too tender from earlier to indulge myself tonight." Sliding his palms up her back, he leaned over and shifted under her torso to cup her breasts as he slid his cock through the seam of her damp folds. "Fuck but you feel good," he groaned with a shudder of pleasure before sinking his teeth into her shoulder.

Tamara shifted her hips against his pelvis. "Then what are you waiting for?"

"Just making sure you're with me." Straightening, Connor used his knees to shove hers further apart while sheathing himself again. With one deep push, he buried himself balls-deep inside her snug pussy, gripping her buttocks to hold her still for another fast ride. "Damn it, Tamara, I swear I'll take you slower next time."

"I don't mind quick," she panted as he plunged in and out of her already grasping channel, her slick heat pulling at his shaft.

"I do, but I'll address that later, much later." His inability to hold back once he was inside her was another sign she'd been right to push past his misgivings about going in this direction. But as he pummeled her depths again, Connor still worried this might be a mistake, that thinking of her as Tamara instead of Tam could muddle his concentration enough he'd screw up somehow, something he'd sworn he would never do again after she'd refused to speak with him the last time.

His balls drew up as prickles of pleasure traversed up his cock. Slipping one hand under her, he rooted out her clit and pressed the delicate piece of swollen flesh against his pumping erection. "Now, Tamara," he demanded.

"Yes, yes, yes," she panted, her orgasm bursting around him as soon as his exploded out of his cockhead.

Connor kept pumping inside her as they collapsed, slowing his thrusts as he savored her tight clasp and ragged breathing. She arched her buttocks against his groin, the plump mounds a soft cushion he could lie on forever. With a deep groan, he pulled out of her, whispering, "Go to sleep, little one."

TAMARA ROLLED OVER, wincing as her well-used body made all its pleasurable aches known. Blinking open blurry eyes, she noted the time on the bedside clock in disbelief. She never slept past eight on the weekend yet here it was after nine and she was still in bed. Too bad she was in here alone. With a yawn, she slid out from under the warm covers and padded into the adjoining bathroom.

The man was insatiable, she groaned, standing under the hot pelting shower. Connor had awoken her in the middle of the night for another go around, surprising her with his stamina. Not that she was complaining. Leaning against the wall, she soaped her body as she recalled every touch, low groan and deep thrust. She'd never indulged in such a sexual marathon, but even if she had, she doubted she would have enjoyed each decadent moment as much as she had relished finally being on the receiving end of Master Con's undivided sexual attention.

But as she dried off and slipped on a pair of jeans and comfortable sweatshirt, morning after uneasiness crept in to put a damper on the lingering pleasure she'd awakened with. Opening the bedroom door, the whiff of coffee that tickled her nose cleared the remaining sleepiness from her head. Passing Amy's empty room, she surmised Con was still here and that pleased her even though she wasn't sure what his mood would be this morning. She doubted he ever felt morning after jitters.

Tamara halted in the still messy dining room as she saw Connor standing at the stove shirtless and shoeless, his brown, sun-streaked hair brushing his shoulders, his back muscles rippling with his arm movements as he stirred eggs. Her breath caught as she gazed at the sexy picture he made, her heart thudding as she prayed he wouldn't do an about-face and end this before it could go any further. Insecurity gripped her and for a moment, she was a kid again, abandoned to a stranger by her mother, waking the next morning afraid the father she'd never known before had changed his mind about having her here.

"I was just about to wake you." Turning, Con held up the spatula, his blue eyes assessing as he gave her a careful once-over. A smile creased his tanned cheeks as his gaze traveled back to her face and he caught the wariness she knew she couldn't hide from him. "The morning after can be a bitch, can't it? Maybe this will help." He strode forward and dropped a soft kiss on her mouth, the touch brief but enough to leave her lips tingling and to cause her heart to roll over.

Tamara gave him a shaky grin. "I don't have as much practice as you with overnighters."

"You'd be surprised. In case you're wondering, other than three monogamous relationships that didn't last beyond a few months, I can count the times I spent the entire night with someone on one hand. Does that help?" he asked, swinging back to the stove.

Compared to her limited encounters, no, but she wouldn't admit that. She looked away from him as she strolled over to the full coffee pot. "I've only had one serious relationship and our split was hard on both of us. I can't imagine going through that three times." She felt sorry for Connor's exes. It must have been difficult for them when he had moved on.

"You planned to marry him. That's a lot more serious than a short affair, during which I made no promises."

She flinched at the reminder but cleared her expression before turning to face him again with a mug in hand. Jeremy was a mistake she would deal with on her own. "I don't want to talk about…" The front door opened, and heat infused Tamara's face as Amy walked in, her stepmother's eyes widening in surprise upon seeing Connor before a beaming smile brightened her face.

"Good morning," she greeted them, not bothering to hide how pleased she was. But when Jason stepped in behind her, it was Connor's turn to look uncomfortable.

After flicking a quick glance towards Tamara, her foreman gave Connor a piercing stare. Following a moment of tense silence, Jason said, "It looks like we weren't the only ones stepping out last night, Amy."

Connor raised a brow and slid the pan of eggs off the burner. "There's enough for all three of you. I have to get going." He cut his eyes to Tamara. "I'll call you later. Amy, Jason, I hope you'll both be at our barbeque next weekend."

Amy jabbed an elbow into Jason's side, and he relaxed his scowl. "We'll be there, Connor. It's been too long since we've all gathered for a fun afternoon."

Tamara had forgotten about the barbeque and now was looking forward to attending even more. "I… uh, I'll walk out with you, Con." She started to follow him back to her room where he'd left his clothes, but he held up a hand and then gave her hair a playful tug. "No need, little one. Eat your breakfast."

"Okay, thanks. Talk to you later." She wished he'd kiss her goodbye but knew he wouldn't with the other two hovering. Getting down plates, she waited until Connor had dressed and she heard him leave before turning to Jason as they sat down at the table. "What gives with the 'daddy glare'?" It was one thing to have the man her father trusted with running the ranch keep an eye out for her as they worked together but quite another to have him go parental on her.

"Sorry." He sighed with a rueful look. "All I could think was what would your father say and acted accordingly."

Amy laughed, reaching over to squeeze Tamara's arm. "We're both fine with Connor and you, just surprised by his sudden change of heart and don't want to see you hurt."

Tamara scooped out the eggs that looked perfect, shaking her head in bemusement over everything that had transpired since she'd arrived home last night from the club. "No more surprised than I was when he showed up here last night." She smiled at Jason. "Thanks for caring, but I'm a big girl. If there's one guy I can handle, it's Connor." At least she hoped that was true. She didn't know what she would do if he decided this change in their relationship wouldn't work and he wanted to go back to 'just friends' status.

Jason nodded, scooping a forkful of scrambled eggs. "As long as he treats you right. The reason I came in was to let you know we checked on the horses since they were so restless last night and found a raccoon inside Lady's stall. I can't figure out how the critter got in there, but it spooked her some. I put her in the corral to settle down, but you might check on her."

"I never heard them, I'm sorry." She couldn't believe she'd slept through the ruckus and blushed when Amy and Jason smirked. Wanting payback, she taunted, "I'm surprised you did."

Amy grunted. "We're not as young as you. And Jason's cabin is closer to the stable."

Scraping her plate clean, Tamara carried it to the sink, replying, "I'm headed out there now to start on the stalls. I'll check on her. Poor thing. I've noticed she gets jittery around smaller animals."

Jason rose and followed her over with his empty dish. "I have a few interviews this morning for Neil's job. I'll let you know if one looks promising enough to hire. I plan to be more selective this time." He sent Amy a wink before strolling out with a wave.

"Okay, give," Amy insisted as soon as he left.

"Me?" Tamara rinsed the plates, cocking her head toward her stepmother. "What about you? Last I heard, you were taking it slow."

Amy shrugged. "What can I say? He wore me down, as, I assume, you did Connor."

"Not so much as wore him down as his brother pointing out the obvious to him, whatever that happened to be. He didn't say a lot, and I was too happy with his change of heart to question him much."

Amy joined her at the counter and started loading the dishwasher. "What's wrong? I can tell by that look on your face something's bothering you."

"I don't know." Tamara sighed, wishing she was as sure of Connor's feelings as she was of her own. "I'm afraid to get my hopes up too soon. He can be stubborn about his protectiveness toward me."

"Well, there are worse traits in a guy."

She thought of Jeremy and admitted that was true. "Yeah, you're right. I'll see you around lunchtime, after I help with chores and take Galahad out."

"I'll be in town all morning, so I'll pick up something to go at the diner," Amy offered, closing the dishwasher and drying her hands.

"Fried chicken for me. Thanks."

Even though Tamara knew Jason would have checked the stable to see where the raccoon might have gotten in, she couldn't help taking a look around herself. Like him, she couldn't locate where the raccoon might have slipped inside once the doors had been shut, but they were wily creatures and could work their way through the tightest gaps. If it happened again, she'd ask Jason to set a trap and then haul the animal far enough away it wouldn't return.

She'd known Lady was a timid mare when she bought her at auction, but she'd been so sweet and in need of a good home after months of neglect by a previous owner, Tamara couldn't resist buying her. As she mucked out the stalls, it bothered her that she hadn't heard the mare's nervous movements and sounds. She'd been so physically drained after Connor finished with her, she doubted an earthquake would have woken her. As exciting as that was for someone who'd never gotten past mediocre in her sexual encounters, seeing to her horse's needs was her responsibility, and one she'd always taken seriously.

Mark, the hand who had been working for the Barton's for over ten years, showed up to help her tackle the eight stalls and by the time they finished, she was more than ready for a breath of fresh air and an invigorating ride. "Thanks for the help, Mark. I hope this didn't put you behind on anything else."

"No, all's fine around here, more so now those damn rustlers have been caught. Did you hear the authorities picked up the other three yesterday?"

"No," she answered, surprised at the news. "Thank goodness. We couldn't afford another loss."

The tall lanky cowboy returned the rakes to the storage room, saying over his shoulder, "I hear you, but we're good. Once Jason hires someone, we can start spreading the herd out further. The pastures are greening up nicely."

"Spring is always welcome. I'm off for a ride. Thanks again."

He lifted his hand in a wave. "Later, Miss."

Mark's good news helped lighten Tamara's mood from fretting over whether Connor would regret coming to her last night. If he did, she'd deal with it, she decided as she swung up on Galahad. Patting his sleek neck, she nudged him into a trot and then a gallop. The smooth bunching of the steed's muscles under her reminded her of Connor's strength and size as he came over her, his thick thighs spreading hers to make room for him. Just one night, that's all he'd given her so far, and she was hooked. No, that wasn't true, she admitted as Galahad took her over the first fence with effortless agility. Spying on Connor and his date that morning at his barn had sealed her fate. Ever since then, she had wanted no one but him in her bed, no matter how hard she'd tried to move on with someone else.

Now that she had what she'd craved for so long, she prayed he wouldn't find an excuse to take it from her.

BY THE TIME dawn broke on the horizon with a glowing yellow-orange sliver Monday morning, Tamara woke up grateful Connor had chosen to return to his place yesterday morning.

He'd surprised her by showing up Saturday and suggesting they stay in instead of going to the club. Just like when she'd been a teenager, they made popcorn and watched a movie. Unlike those times, as soon as Amy left for Jason's, he'd stripped her and taken her on the floor, then bent over the couch and again in her bed where he had insisted, she ride him for a change. And she'd loved every second of his rough, demanding possession even though her body ached from the unaccustomed activity all day yesterday.

He'd called yesterday, but a problem with a well had kept him tied up until late and she spent most of the day helping to repair a line of fencing someone knocked down the night before. Jason guessed kids had likely been out causing trouble, drinking and driving through the fields without paying attention. Whoever they'd been, they'd managed to destroy yards of fencing along one side of their most used pasture during this time of year. Between rounding up the escaped cattle and repair work, she'd been exhausted last night, but had still missed him wrapped around her.

Because she was on uneven footing over whether his change of heart would last, she refrained from mentioning the downed fence when he'd asked how her day was going. He was expert at finding things to worry about her on his own, and there wasn't anything he could do about reckless kids causing damage. After a quick shower and cup of coffee, she drove into the clinic, eager to see him again even if it would be for his last therapy appointment. Maybe they could meet up for lunch on the days she worked at the clinic, she thought as she parked and entered the therapy room. When he arrived a few minutes later, her heart thudded and her body throbbed as if she hadn't seen him in weeks instead of one day and she knew if he ended up regretting their intimacy, it would hurt worse than any other painful experience of her life.

CONNOR DIDN'T CARE for change in his life. He liked the way things were and had never desired a shake-up in the status quo. Why mess with a good thing? But he knew he was in for a big one when he'd found himself missing Tam's soft, toned body curled against his last night after spending the two previous nights in her bed. As he entered the physical therapy room, she looked up at him with the same vulnerable, insecure expression she'd worn when her father had arrived at the fair riding ring to pick her up all those years ago, the same expression she couldn't hide the other morning following their first night together. A tight clutch gripped his chest and a surge of encompassing warmth spread through his body. It had always been his job to see to her needs, whatever they were, and it was both a heady and scary feeling to discover the idea of change appealed to him now because it was Tam the change revolved around.

He still harbored reservations about entering this new phase of their relationship – old habits were difficult to set aside in just one weekend – but damned if he didn't find himself wanting to explore where these newfound, expanded feelings would take them, starting with easing the look of uncertainty on her expressive face.

"Good morning, little one," he greeted her, hanging up his hat as she returned his smile.

"Hey." Coming around her desk, he could see her pulse flutter in her neck as her look changed to one he was hard-pressed to ignore.

"Careful, *Tamara*," Connor warned with emphasis on her full name. "You're the one who doesn't want me placing you in a compromising position here at work."

She giggled and his grin widened. "I can't help it. You've turned me into a hussy. I missed you yesterday."

Running his fingers down her flushed cheek, he was relieved to see the return of her confidence as he leaned down and brushed her mouth with his. "I missed you, too. Now," stepping back from temptation, he asked, "what torture are you planning for me today? And remember, I have ways of getting even."

"I like the ways you torture me," Tamara admitted, leading him to the raised mat. "Sit down and I'll check your progress. I'm already pretty sure you can use it as much as you want, so long as you don't overdo." The look he gave her had her shaking her head with a rueful sigh. "I know, you've already been doing as much as you want, so I don't know why I even bother."

"Because you know me," Connor returned, enjoying her hands on him any way he could get them. "Were you and Amy able to spend time together yesterday?"

She hesitated and then said, "Some. We're still shorthanded, so I've been helping out as much as I can when I'm not here."

"I thought Jason had a few prospects for hiring."

"He does, and I think he's contacting someone today, so that will help. Our herd is down, with the ones we just sold at market and the stolen cattle, so the work's been doable. I hear the authorities have caught the rest of the thieves."

"Just the other day. They also located several head they hadn't disposed of yet. It's the same gang that worked out of Wyoming last year, so there are a lot of ranchers breathing a sigh of relief now." She released his arm and he stood, itching to put his hands on her. Too bad he couldn't indulge himself here. "Come early to the barbeque next Saturday and, if you're interested, I'll show you a few calves I can give you."

Her mouth tightened and those gray eyes flashed, a stubborn reaction he expected to follow his offer. "You mean you'll *sell* them to me, right?"

"Sure, sweetie, whatever you say." Her glare went to slits, but before she could snap at him for calling her sweetie again, he asked, "Am I good to go, then?" Rotating his shoulder, he gave her one of his most endearing grins.

Tamara smacked his arm, her lips twitching. "Go, and don't call me sweetie."

Connor strolled out whistling even though he still worried taking Tam to his bed would end up being another mistake, and he couldn't risk losing her again. The years she'd kept herself from him had been the most difficult of his life. The next time he screwed up she might not forgive him and a life without Tam in it wasn't worth thinking about. God forbid if taking this step ever interfered with his need to always see to her happiness and safety.

Chapter 11

"No, absolutely not, Jeremy." Tamara tightened her hand on the phone as she tried her best to keep calm. Telling herself she'd done wrong by her ex wasn't working any longer. She needed to get him to move on. "I told you last week when you showed up uninvited I didn't want to see you. Do not come back. Why haven't you returned to Boise?" She made sure her frustration level came through loud and clear.

"I don't understand why you keep choosing that place, with all its problems, over the much easier life I can offer you. That just doesn't make sense, baby."

Jeremy's own annoyance bled through the line, which worked to further irk her. She now realized what a mistake it had been to mention the problems plaguing the ranch this week. At first, she'd used the early morning call from the sheriff telling them their cattle had gotten loose and were wandering along the highway and the second episode with that damn raccoon getting into the stable and going right for Lady's stall to terrify the poor mare as an excuse not to meet up with Jeremy to talk. But this morning, when she and Amy had discovered the new bag of pelleted horse feed she'd just picked up had been bug infested, put her in no mood to deal with his continued obstinance, regardless of her guilt over their relationship.

"I don't know how I can be any clearer, Jeremy. I love this ranch, despite the problems that go with the territory. I've apologized for our split so many times, I can't think of another way to say it. We're through, I am not coming back, neither to Boise nor to you. Please, go home and move on with your life and do not contact me again, for any reason. For the last time, goodbye."

She hung up before he could say anything else, tears pricking her eyes. From his behavior this week, no one would believe he was a nice guy, one who didn't deserve a woman whose feelings were lukewarm, at best. It hadn't been easy, but she'd kept her troubles with her ex and the extra work around the ranch from mishaps that kept popping up from Connor. Even though they'd gotten together every day this past week and he'd shown her how inventive he could be in carving out time and a place for a quickie that left her shaking with satisfaction in more ways than one, their relationship was still too new and fragile to burden it with problems she was perfectly capable of handling on her own.

He had his own hands full working the Dunbar spread and prepping for the barbeque she was looking forward to attending this afternoon, even more so after he'd opted to spend last night alone with her instead of going to the club again after Amy announced she would be at Jason's all night. His refusal to stay the night in her bed with her stepmother down the hall tickled her with his sense of honor. Tamara had to admit she enjoyed the evenings alone with him as much as she had socializing and playing at The Barn.

But Connor hadn't said a word or given her a hint about where they might be headed, or about his feelings now that they were a couple. His determination to remain footloose and free of committed entanglements his entire adult life couldn't be discounted in one short week, especially given his reluctance to enter into this relationship in the first place.

"Jeremy again?" Amy asked, coming into the kitchen as Tamara tossed her phone on the table.

"Yes, but I'm hoping I was blunt enough to send him back home."

"You've been blunt before," Amy reminded her as she pulled the large bowl of potato salad from the refrigerator.

"I know, but I keep hoping one of these times it'll get through to him. I still can't believe he just showed up here last week. I never dreamed he would be that desperate to get back together." The oven buzzed and Tamara retrieved the batch of dark chocolate brownies she'd made for the barbeque.

"Hopefully, he'll give up now." Amy eyed the brownies with hunger, taking a deep, appreciative whiff. "Oh, those smell wonderful. Are you riding over with Jason and me?"

"Yes, that'll be easiest. Connor can bring me back, or I might go to his place. I'll let you know. Thank goodness Jason hired a new hand this week. He's assigned him and Mark to keep an eye on things while we're gone since everyone else will be at the barbeque. Let's hope this run of bad luck has ended."

"There have been an unusual number of problems. What did you think of Jason's suggestion someone might be screwing with us?"

Leaning against the counter, Tamara sighed at the possibility kids were behind all of the problems. "There's always that to consider. Teenagers get bored."

Amy's lips twitched. "Yes, I remember."

"Hey, I was a good kid." She smiled back.

"Yes, you were, but Connor helped keep you that way and stepped in before you could get yourself in too much trouble," Amy reminded her.

"His overprotectiveness did put a crimp in my fun."

"But he's worth it?"

Tamara's smile split her face. "Oh, yeah." At least, she prayed he would continue to be.

Laughing, Amy grabbed the bowl and turned toward the door, hearing Jason's truck pull up out front. "Let's go before he comes looking for us."

Over fifty friends and neighbors were gathered on the sweeping lawn surrounding Caden's home. Tamara used to love riding over here when she'd been younger and hanging out with Connor while he worked. Now, she mused as she got out of Jason's truck, she much preferred hanging out at Connor's house, and staying the night in his bed over watching him work. Although, as she caught sight of him leaning on a rail at the horse corral, his tight jeans stretched across his backside, a pair of chaps framing his pelvis and his Stetson shading his rough-hewn face, there was definitely something to be said about taking a moment to ogle him now.

"Here, I'll take your brownies over to the food table. Jason can carry the potato salad. You go on," Amy offered after seeing where Tamara's gaze had landed.

"Thanks. Catch you later." Tamara handed Amy her pan and took off toward the corral, spotting Avery, Sydney and Nan standing opposite the guys.

She waved to people she knew as she passed the long tables and small gatherings. One of the hands led a pony carrying a toddler around in circles, the sight reminding her of her first horseback ride, and the beginning of her special relationship with Connor. For the first time since he'd driven her away with his hurtful words five years ago, she allowed herself to feel a glimmer of hope they were heading for a future that would be as special, if not more so.

With a loud *whoop*, Caden bounced on top of a bucking bronco, keeping his seat with a tight grip on the reins and pommel. "You'd think they would be getting too old for this," Tamara drawled as she settled next to Nan at the rail and leaned her arms on the top post. Her eyes slid across the dusty corral to Connor, who returned her smile with a thumbs-up gesture as

Caden managed to slow the horse's efforts down enough to jump off with a wide grin of accomplishment. Connor hopped the fence to take his turn on the unbroken steed, slapping his brother on the back as he taunted him with a laugh. "Too much for you, old man? Watch how it's done."

Nan smiled, shaking her head as Caden flipped Connor the bird. "I don't think they'll ever consider themselves too old to play. Damn, they make a nice picture, don't they?" She nodded to where Caden swung over the fence, joining Grayson and Dan outside the corral as Connor settled onto the back of the quivering horse, both appearing eager to see who would win this round.

"One I never get tired of," Sydney stated from Nan's left. "Who doesn't love a cowboy strolling around in chaps with his hat tipped to keep his expression a secret?"

Avery nodded from the end. "Makes them both sexy and mysterious."

"Panty-melting." Nan fanned herself.

Connor's laugh rang out as he took off his hat and swung it in a circle above his head. The horse slowed his efforts and it didn't take but a few more minutes of him working the steed with a combination of strong control and coaxing words to calm the bronco enough he could dismount safely.

"Whoa, girlfriend, I know that look," Nan said as Connor glanced her way while stroking the jittery horse, his grin still cocky, the slit of his eyes, just visible beneath the brim of his lowered hat, lit with a blue flame. "We expected to see you two last night at The Barn."

Tamara grew warm, pleased and excited he wasn't hiding the shift in their relationship from anyone. The insecure part of her who had waited for years to get him to see her as more than a friend had worried he would want to keep their new relationship between them as he continued to think it over. She'd been only too eager to spill the beans to her friends when they'd met up for their weekly tea, knowing she had their support.

"He wanted to stay in. I forgot to ask. Did you get in trouble for covering for me last week?" Dragging her eyes away from Connor, Tamara cast her friend a worried look as Nan grimaced with a rueful smile.

"Uh, yeah a little. Master Connor left it up to Master Dan. But, don't fret." Nan laughed, waving an airy hand. "You know me. I loved every swat."

Sydney leaned around Nan, saying, "Boy, did she. There's no way you'd catch me letting Caden lock me in that medieval torture device and giving anyone interested the chance to whack my butt as they walked by."

Tamara winced. "Torture device?"

"Stocks. A new purchase the guys are way too excited over," Avery answered. "I got off easy." A flush stole over her face. "Master Grayson gave me my punishment himself."

"I can see that was okay with you, Avery, but Nan, your punishment sounds awful." Tamara shuddered at the thought of such a public, painful humiliation.

"It wasn't." Nan smirked. "Master Dan made every swat worth my while afterward. Man, that guy can fuck."

They all burst out laughing because, really, who could argue with such logic?

"What's so funny, or do we want to know?" Connor interrupted as he and Caden strolled over.

"Oh, you'd love to know, but it's girl stuff, so, not telling." Sydney took Caden's outstretched hand and hopped off the fence.

"Come on." Caden tugged her next to him. "I have to start the grill and grab a burger before I run out serving them to everyone else, and I'm more than ready for a large scoop of those homemade fries I smelled you making all morning."

"We'll catch up with you shortly. Tamara and I are up at the pony rides."

Several eyes swung Connor's way at his use of her full name, and it was Tamara's turn to blush as Grayson joined them with a crooked grin around the toothpick nestled in the corner of his mouth. "Tamara?"

With a shrug, Connor looked at her. "Ask her. She's the one who insisted we were past nicknames."

When he phrased it that way, it did sound dumb. "Hey, I just wanted him to quit seeing me as a kid," she defended herself before flicking Con a sheepish glance. "But I kind of have to admit I miss you calling me Tam."

He draped his arm around her shoulders and steered her toward the pony ring, saying loud enough for everyone to hear, "You can always dress up as a school girl when you want to hear your nickname again."

"I GOT ONE!"

Connor grinned at Tam's squeal as she gripped her new fishing pole with both hands and struggled against the yank on the line from under the water. "Okay, Tam, reel it in, nice and slow, just like I showed you."

Her little face scrunched with a now familiar look of determination as she pulled up on the line. He moved behind her and could feel her small, eleven-year-old body shaking with her excitement and efforts. "Look at that, you've landed a nice-sized brown trout. Way to go, sweetie." He tugged her long black braid and got a beaming smile in return that lit up her gray eyes. "Let's toss it in the bucket and head back for your birthday dinner."

She looked at the flopping fish on the bank and shook her head. "No way, Con. I'm tossing the poor guy back in." She reached for the trout and wrinkled her nose at the slimy feel. "Uh, you do it."

He caught the fish she thrust at him with a laugh. "Wimp. Watch, this is how you remove the hook." He gave her a quick lesson and then flung the fish back in the pond with a teasing grin. "There. Safe from the grill for another day. Come on. I want cake."

She took his hand with a look of gratitude. "Me too."

Connor glanced over at Tam as she squealed and brought in her catch, the look on her face this afternoon the same as the first time he'd taught her to fish in this same pond. This fishing contest was just one of the activities going on as their friends and neighbors mingled and enjoyed Caden's labors at the grill. Connor and Tam had already helped give pony rides to the kids and participated on opposite sides of a volleyball game before entering the fishing contest. Setting his own pole down, he strode over to her, admiring her skill in reeling in the large trout wiggling on her line.

"You may have the winner there, Tamara." Damn but it was difficult to remember she now preferred he used her full name instead of the abbreviated nickname he was the only one to ever call her. He wasn't surprised when she wrinkled her nose as she pulled the hook from the trout's throat and placed it on the scale. It was the same cute expression she'd worn when she'd handled her first fish. "Thirty-five inches. That's definitely a contender."

"It's been ages since I've gone fishing." Picking up the trout by its tail fin, she tossed it back into the two-acre pond.

"That hasn't changed," he drawled, tugging on her braid. He was glad her hair was still long enough to plait. "Your catches never have made it to the grill."

"And never will. What do you want to do next?" She looked up at him with a beaming smile, her eyes alight with expectation. Connor's thoughts shifted to the lustful intentions he'd planned for some time today.

Despite feeling good after getting a handle on the new bronco they'd picked up at auction and the fun he'd been having with Tamara, he couldn't help the constant frissons of uneasiness over their new relationship that wouldn't let go. Everything had gone so well this past week, both with the ranch and with Tam. With Greg and Devin's additional purchases of his and Caden's horse stock for their new dude ranch, their stock was down and they had buyers lined up, waiting. With luck, the new stud could be used soon to increase their inventory and the extra income would keep rolling in. If only he could be as sure he'd made the right decision in taking the step she'd wanted for so long as he was about his and Caden's decision to go into horse breeding, he would feel a lot better about it.

But today, he was determined to take advantage of the pleasant afternoon, the good food and then the distraction of everyone eating to sneak away with his girl. "I'm hungry for another burger and we haven't hit the buffet and desserts yet." He'd downed one before coming out to the pond, but Tamara had opted to wait.

"That doesn't surprise me. You're always hungry," she returned as she took his hand.

Connor squeezed her hand and leaned down to whisper in her ear. "I'm not just hungry for food." He nipped the small lobe before pulling back with a teasing grin at her flushed face. "But food first."

WITH AN EAGER STEP, Tamara followed Connor over to the grill where Caden placed a juicy hamburger on her plate before they visited the buffet table. She, too, was hungry for more than food, which had been the case this whole week whenever they were together. Like an addict craving his next fix, she couldn't get enough of his attention and she knew a part of her desperate need stemmed from not knowing when or if this would end.

As they took a seat next to Avery and Grayson and Connor rested his left hand on the inside of her thigh, she shoved aside those worries for another day. So far, today was perfect.

"I didn't know what to take. Everything looked wonderful," she said, glancing down at her full plate with a rueful grimace.

"I'll eat what you don't," Connor offered, squeezing her leg.

A ripple of heat coursed up Tamara's leg to her crotch and it took every ounce of willpower she possessed not to tighten her thighs around his hand.

Avery shook her head, looking down at her own stacked plate. "Grayson's responsible for mine. I've been trying to lose weight." She sent him a mock glare from behind her dark-rimmed glasses.

"You don't need to drop a pound. I like all of your soft curves. Eat." The warm look in Grayson's gray-green eyes belied his stern, gruff voice.

"Can't argue with that."

Connor winked at Avery and talk turned to horses as Tamara and Avery rolled their eyes. By the time Tamara couldn't shovel in another bite, the table had filled up and she was ready to move again. Thankfully, Connor was of like mind as he stood and gathered their plates with a nod to their friends.

"We're going for a walk. Catch you guys later."

After dumping their plates in a trash bin, he snatched her hand and whisked her toward the barns, and she didn't question him. With him was where she wanted to be; it didn't matter where. As he led her down a path and away from the people and activities, her heartbeat ratcheted up a notch, her body going on high alert.

Curiosity prompted her to ask, "Where are we going?" as they passed a copse of trees that blocked them from view and he tugged her toward a small barn she hadn't seen before. "Is that new?"

"Fairly. It's our calf barn, for the ones who need extra care or have special needs." Connor pulled open a side door and the mingling scents of hay and manure wafted out to tickle her senses.

"And you're showing me this now, why?" She flicked him a look of curiosity and the intent she read on his face tossed her straight into lust.

"I owe you a punishment for taking off last week that I haven't gotten around to delivering yet. This way."

Connor urged her toward a storeroom and Tamara stumbled after him, stuttering on a laugh. "*Now? Here?*"

"Oh, yeah, now, and here." Closing the door behind him, he yanked her against his muscled body and swooped down to take her mouth in a searing kiss.

Tamara sank against his hard frame, relishing the tight band of his arm wrapping around her hips, pressing her closer to his pelvis as he delved between her lips to duel with her tongue. She moaned, thrusting against the hard, promising bulge he ground against her mound. By the time he loosened his hold and pulled back, she was ready for whatever he wanted. At least, she thought so until she glimpsed the blanket covered sawhorse and the horse grooming mitt-brush sitting on the hay bale next to it.

"You don't think you're going to use that on me, do you?" She flipped him an incredulous glance, her rapid pulse sending her blood rushing through her veins in a heated gush. One side of the mitt was covered with PVC brush bristles, the other, a pimpled rubber surface used to massage. She could only imagine how each side would differ in sensation if applied to her backside.

"No, I know I am." His hands went to the waist of her jeans as he grinned at her from under the brim of his lowered hat. "Didn't I tell you to wait for me last time we were at the club?" Connor lowered the zipper and tugged her jeans down to mid-thigh. "And did you deliberately disobey my instructions, with your friend's help?" Her panties followed, leaving her standing there bare-assed in a swath of sunlight streaming in through the one window.

Excitement curled low in Tamara's belly, her nipples puckering as she replied on a rushed breath, "You were an ass."

"I was looking out for your well-being, like always. Like I'm doing now." Connor spun her around and pushed her over the sawhorse until her hips were resting atop it, leaving her upper body to dangle over the side as she braced on her toes.

Reaching out to steady herself, she exclaimed, "Connor! I can't stay like this!"

He brushed a hand over her clenching cheeks as he chided her. "Now, Tamara. Have I ever let you fall?"

Tamara felt his other hand press on her lower back, a supportive touch that calmed her until he swatted her buttock. Even expecting it, she jumped, her breath bursting from her lungs in a *whoosh* as the painful sting warmed her everywhere. She tried wriggling her hips, whether to escape the next blistering smack or embrace it, she wasn't sure, but the brace of his hand was enough to hold her still.

"Now, aren't you sorry you didn't stay put like I instructed?" He slapped her again, a little harder, the pain a touch sharper, the encompassing warmth a degree hotter.

Dangling face down kept her from trying to look back up at him, but she shook her head in denial. "No. You walked away after…" Tamara paused to suck in a gasp as he delivered a volley of quick, hard swats that covered her entire backside before pausing to slip on the red grooming mitt. "Con," she groaned, shaking from the light stroke of PVC bristles scraping over her throbbing flesh.

"That's Master Con, little one," he reminded her, the smile in his voice warming her in a different way. She did love his teasing side. "Your pretty red ass is too tempting. I think you've had enough." He scraped the bristles once more over her buttocks before turning the mitt around and soothing the ache with the softer massage side, gliding over her tortured flesh and spreading tingles down her legs. "See? Not so bad, is it?" Not sparing an inch of her entire, upturned butt, the small nodules left behind small tremors in their wake that increased her ache for his rough possession.

"Not now," she admitted, the pain subsiding as fast as he'd initiated it, leaving her buttocks to pulse softly.

"I love your honesty." Connor pulled off the mitt and tossed it onto the hay before dragging one finger up her wet seam. "And how you respond to me, no matter what I do to your delectable body." With a laugh of pure pleasure that gave Tamara a warm fuzzy feeling, he lifted her, yanked her jeans down further and helped her work her right leg free of the denim without removing her sneaker.

"Now," she demanded, throwing her arms around his broad shoulders, desperate to feel him thrusting inside her again. "Leave on your hat."

He chuckled and followed her down onto the hay bale, one hand going to his zipper. "Yes, ma'am. Anything to please."

It took just seconds before his heated flesh sprung free against her bare leg, her breathing turning to heavy pants as he sheathed himself then spread her thighs by settling his hips between them. Tamara lifted her leg around his lower back as he thrust into her welcoming body, her copious juices making it easy for him to bury himself to the hilt. "Oh God," she groaned as he reared back and plunged forward again without pause.

"You said now. I'm just giving you want you want," Connor rasped above her mouth before molding his lips over hers again, swallowing her next low moan.

Her hips bucked against his marauding shaft, her body shaking as flames of rippling heat spread straight up her pussy. She wondered if she would ever get enough of him, and then thought of nothing else except the pleasure spiraling her headlong to that plane where nothing mattered except the sweeping ecstasy only he had ever brought her to.

Connor released her mouth as his cock jerked with his

orgasm, his breathless curse mingling with her cry. Putting his mouth to her ear as he ground into her, his quiet laugh reverberated in her head. "Be quiet unless you want to draw a crowd," he panted.

Tamara bit her lip, basking in the way his cock stretched and filled her, in the spasms continuing to engulf her from head to toe, in his pleasure and amusement. Nothing had ever been this good, nothing could be. There was no one but Con, could never be anyone else. As he eased back, she kept her eyes closed, hoping to hear him say this was going where she wanted it to, afraid to read nothing more on his face than the sated pleasure and fondness he'd been showing her all week.

CONNOR PULLED from Tam's snug heat, groaning as her slick muscles continued to clench along his withdrawal. *Jesus*. Would he ever get enough of her? He shook his head at the thought that had never entered his mind with any other woman, listening to make sure no one had taken it upon themselves to either follow them or had the same idea as he when he'd planned this little diversion. Other than the calves moving around their stalls and the occasional low bawling, all was quiet except for their labored breathing.

Shifting to her side, he ran a hand over her quivering stomach, smiling down at her flushed face and closed eyes as her chest rose and fell with her heavy breathing. His chest tightened, as it always did when he gazed at her after they'd made love, but fear of losing her still clogged his throat, stalling the words he knew he should say. Instead, he pinched her chin and quipped lightly, "Are you going to make it, little one?"

Her lids lifted slowly, and he found himself drowning in the glazed depths of her pewter eyes. "Maybe. I'm not sure yet." She wiggled, grimacing as her buttocks scraped over the scratchy hay. "Oh, that wasn't smart."

Connor chuckled and gave Tamara a quick kiss before standing. "We better get back." He disposed of the condom in a corner trash bin and turned to see her pulling her jeans back up over that delectable, red ass. With a sigh, he reined in the urge to fill his hands with those tempting globes and test the lingering warmth. "Tam…" Connor started toward her and then froze as the faint clang of a bell drifted through the barn walls. "*Shit.* Come on, let's…" His phone buzzed and he yanked it out of his pocket, seeing Caden's number. Dread had him gripping Tam's elbow and steering her outside as he barked into the phone, "What's up?"

"That's the fire alarm from Barton's. Where are you?" Caden snapped with urgency.

"We went for a walk, we're on our way back." Connor's gaze sliced down at Tam and he could tell she heard his brother's bad news. He listened to Caden a minute more before hanging up.

"It's my place?" Her voice quivered but she didn't slow her steps as they dashed back toward the house.

Connor nodded with regret. "One of your hands called Jason. A fire in one of the barns. He and Amy are already on their way back and others are following. Let's hurry."

He prayed her employees had it under control before it spread or did too much damage. The warning bells a lot of the ranchers had worked well in sending out a fast plea for help in situations like this, where every second counted if both livestock and buildings were going to be saved. The Barton ranch abutted theirs, close enough everyone heard the bell and acted without hesitation in hightailing it over there. *Everything is going to be fine*, he kept telling himself as he ushered her into his truck and took off for her place, leaving behind only a few of the older neighbors to clean up what they could of the remnants of the barbeque.

Chapter 12

Tamara had gone cold from head to toe the moment she heard Caden's voice over the phone, the word 'fire' causing fear to block all rational thought. As soon as Connor pulled in front of her house and she saw the flames licking up the side of the stable, her heart lodged in her throat and terror for her beloved stallion and the other horses put a stranglehold on her emotions. She flew out of the truck the moment he stopped, never hearing his shout for her to wait. As she dashed across the wide lawn, she never saw her friends and neighbors working together to pump water from the well onto the fire, didn't hear the wail of sirens as the volunteer fire truck roared up the drive and didn't think about her own safety as she ran into the stable and was met with a stifling wall of heat.

Gasping, she shielded her eyes against the stinging smoke and almost crumpled to the ground in relief when she saw the empty stalls. Coughing, she spotted Mark right before he took her arm and ushered her toward the back.

"We've got it under control, but the structure isn't safe," he said, handing her his kerchief to hold over her nose and mouth as they stumbled back outside.

Blinking her eyes against the watery blur, Tamara made out the wavery forms of her horses grazing in the pasture, at least a mile away. Galahad's silver-white coat stood out among the brown and black shades of the other horses. "Thank God." She coughed, her hands shaking in relief. "Where's Jason? What… what happened?"

Before Mark could answer, Connor's furious voice blasted her from behind. "Goddamn it, Tam! What were you thinking?" Wrapping his hands around her upper arms, he hauled her against him and up on her toes until they were nose to nose. "You just took ten years off my life," he growled in a voice that shook with more than anger.

"I'm sorry, I wasn't thinking. I had to make sure they were okay. Galahad, he's…" Tamara choked up, her eyes filling with tears as she imagined losing the precious gift from her father in such a horrendous way, a gift that had meant so much at a critical time in her life.

Connor sighed and hugged her, the rapid beat of his heart under her ear a soothing balm for her own out of control, staccato rhythm. The shouts from people banding together to help them out finally reached her ears, as did the sizzle of doused flames. The scent of charred wood stung her nose, but the stable remained standing and she prayed the damage was limited to the one side.

"Mark," Con said from above her head, "what do you know?"

"It's definitely arson. I spotted an ex-employee taking off as soon as I smelled smoke but couldn't give chase until I got the horses out. I sent Jason out looking for him as soon as he arrived since he brought plenty of help."

Tamara pulled away from Connor as the three of them started walking around to the front, having a good idea who Mark saw. "It was Neil Anders, wasn't it?"

"Yeah, I'm afraid so. In fact, there they are now." Mark

nodded and Tamara turned to see Sheriff Monroe and Jason leading her handcuffed, disgraced ex-employee their way.

Before she could say anything, Grayson leveled his steely-eyed gaze on her and asked in his quiet, authoritative tone, "You want to tell me why you haven't reported the vandalism going on around here, sugar?"

She felt Connor stiffen next to her and dreaded his response to the sheriff's disclosure. This was not going to sit well with him.

"What vandalism?"

The very softness of Connor's tone sent a shiver of unease down Tamara's spine even before she looked up and saw him glaring in accusation at her. Jason also frowned as he added his two cents.

"You didn't tell him about the raccoon, downed fencing, tainted feed or loose cattle?" Her foreman cuffed a sullen Neil on the back of his head. "The trouble he's been causing."

Tamara tried not to think about the way Connor shifted away from her or his sudden silence as she asked, "Neil, why?"

"Don't blame me," he snapped. "It was your boyfriend's idea. If I hadn't needed the money he offered after you canned me, none of this would have happened."

"Sounds like a confession to me. Come on, asshole. Let's get you booked and you can give me this other guy's name," Grayson said.

"It was Jeremy Hines, wasn't it? And he's not my boyfriend, hasn't been for months." Tamara couldn't believe Jeremy would go to such extremes, but from the closed look on Connor's face, she had more important concerns to deal with right now.

EVERY MUSCLE in Connor's body went taut with anger, disbelief and concern as he faced one of his worst nightmares. The fear that had gripped him when Tam had jumped out of his truck and run into the burning stable before he could stop her still threatened to choke him. To stand here and hear she had kept such vital information from him this past week regarding incidents that could have, at any time, impacted her safety reminded him of all the reasons he never should have succumbed to the temptation and her insistence they expand their relationship. All the while he'd been fucking her, those two men had been waging a personal vendetta against her that could have cost her so much more than damage to her property.

Connor looked down at Tam and his heart constricted at the soot on her cheek and the resignation in her eyes. She knew, even before he said the words, their short jaunt into an intimate relationship was over.

"Connor… Con, please listen," she pleaded, reaching out for him.

He stepped back before she could touch him, his anger with her slipping out along with his anxiety as he stated, "No, Tam. You should have told me what was going on. My God, if anything had happened to you… if they'd hurt you in any way…" He couldn't finish. His throat tightened at just the thought of harm coming to her, harm he failed to prevent or rescue her from because his fucking little head had taken over. "It was a mistake to give in to you regarding our relationship. We can't continue as we have been this week. You'll see I'm right."

Connor turned from her stricken face and took long, ground stomping strides towards Grayson's cruiser, vibrating with the need to relieve his tension and fury with physical exertion.

"Hold up, Grayson," he called out before the sheriff could usher Tam's tormenter into his vehicle.

"Problem?" Grayson asked, keeping a grip on his sullen prisoner's upper arm as he faced Connor.

"Nothing this won't help." He didn't hold back as he plowed a fist into Anders' midsection, the punk doubling over on a gasp as Grayson kept him from crumpling to the ground with his tight hold.

"Feel better?" Grayson drawled as Neil straightened by slow degrees, his face flushed with anger and pain.

"No." Connor got in Neil's face and snarled, "I'm going to let the sheriff handle you and your accomplice, but if either of you show your face around here again once you get your asses out of jail, you'll get more than that one punch. Got it?"

Neil struggled with his breath as he wheezed, "That... that's assault. I... I'm charg... charging..."

"I didn't see anything," Grayson interjected. "Did you, Connor?"

"Not a fucking thing." With a grateful nod to his friend, he pivoted and saw Amy and Tam distributing water bottles to the volunteers as the fire truck rumbled its way back to the highway. Smoke still drifted up from the charred side of the structure, but all the flames appeared to be out. He jumped in to help Caden and Dan put away hoses, a heaviness weighing his shoulders down that had nothing to do with his old injury or the work involved in setting as much of the Barton property back to rights as they could for now.

One week later

Tamara ran the brush over Galahad's smooth flank, the big steed's muscles rippling under her stroking hand. With the warm afternoon sun beating down on her back, a fresh breeze bringing the scent of spring and her beloved pet giving her his unconditional loyalty and support, she could almost set aside the tension of the past few days. Almost was as close as she'd come though. She'd always found grooming her favorite horse to be soothing therapy for when she was upset, but this fun chore failed to settle her mind even if it did ease the tightness in her shoulders. She wasn't surprised. Nothing she'd tried this past week had worked to dispel her despondency over Connor's change in their relationship or her exasperation with his stubbornness. He hadn't called or come by, but she'd seen him every day, riding along the fences separating their property, keeping a vigilant watch on her and a constant lookout for trouble.

According to Sheriff Monroe, as part of a plea bargain, Neil confessed to aiding the rustlers by passing on information and even assisting by calling in sick when he was scheduled to watch, making it easy for them to grab those last few Barton cattle and would testify against them. When he was let go, he lost both his job and the payments from the cattle thieves, making him desperate to take the money Jeremy offered. He was still looking at jail time for arson and destruction of property and Jeremy would likely plea bargain out. Her ex had returned to Boise after she'd refused to take his calls. As far as she knew, he'd gotten the message when she'd given a statement against him to Grayson, outlining his harassment of her since their split. She didn't know what the full extent of the legal consequences would be for either Jeremy or Neil's actions, and at this point, didn't care so long as they paid in some way for what they did.

Shifting around Galahad's rear quarters, she smoothed the brush over his other side, the soft butt of his head to her shoulder drawing her smile. "Yeah, yeah, I know. You want your treat and a ride. Almost done, big guy."

Tamara heard Amy's footsteps before she peered over Galahad's back and saw her stepmother approaching the corral. Amy had been hovering with maternal concern for the last six days, staying at the house every night instead of Jason's place. She'd planned to shoo her out tonight, but from the glint of determination in her eyes, Amy might have already decided it was time she quit babying Tamara.

"I just got a call from the contractor and they'll be out here first thing Monday morning. He said they should have the stable repairs done within a few days," Amy said as she stepped up to Galahad's head and stroked his velvety nose.

"Good. I'll feel better when we can stable the horses at night again. Want to go for a ride with me?" Tamara set the brush down on a bench and reached for the saddle blanket draped over the rail.

"No, but thanks. Jason and I are going into town for an early dinner." Cocking her head, Amy surprised her by suggesting, "You should go to the club tonight instead of sitting at home, pining for Connor. It might push him into coming around sooner."

Funny, Tamara mused. Nan, Sydney and Avery had said the same thing when she'd joined them at the teashop a few days ago. Unlike all of her well-meaning friends and family, she knew Connor's stubbornness outweighed hers when it came to their relationship.

Shaking her head, she replied with a sigh, "I doubt it, Amy. I'm sure after my big mistake of keeping quiet about the trouble around here that led to the fire, he's dug in his heels. Besides, the thought of going out, being with someone else… I just don't want to."

"Fine, but if it were me, I'd quit letting that man dictate my life. You already let him drive you away for five years. How much more time are you going to give him?"

Amy pivoted and walked away without another word, but it only took Tamara a few moments to consider her words and conclude she was right. If Con wanted to go back to 'just friends' then fine. She wouldn't waste any more time or energy on the man. She ignored the tight squeeze around her heart as she saddled Galahad and swung up. It would do no good to continue to fret over what she couldn't change or wish he would change. With a heeled nudge to her steed's sides, they took off across the sweeping meadow as she tried to work up as much enthusiasm for going to the club tonight as she had for the ride.

CONNOR PULLED up on Dusty's reins and brought the Palomino to a stop so he could take a moment and watch Tam riding. Bent low over Galahad's neck, her black hair flying out behind her and her toned thighs gripping the steed's heaving sides, the two blazed a trail across the wide expanse of pasture. It was a scene he never tired of looking upon.

Every time he thought of the potential harm she could have come to this past week while he'd had his head in the clouds fucking her, his body shook with fear. Losing her was not an option, and if that meant going back to their previous relationship then that was a sacrifice he was willing to make. But, damn, it had been hard, harder than he'd ever imagined. He missed her. Not just her delectable body wrapped around his every night, but the return of their easy comradery, hearing her voice every day, seeing the smile that lit her gray eyes to a silver sheen. All the things he'd missed so much when she'd lived in Boise and refused to talk to him, and he'd grown accustomed to enjoying again.

Nudging Dusty, he rode along the fence line, his job today to look for repairs that needed to get done. He wasn't surprised to see Caden riding up; his brother had been nagging him daily over this latest rift between him and Tam, calling him everything from a stubborn fool to a pigheaded jackass. Because Caden was right didn't change the fact he hadn't been there for Tam when he'd needed to be, that he'd dropped his guard while fucking her. For his peace of mind, he couldn't afford to make that mistake again.

"Find anything?" Caden asked as he pulled alongside Connor.

"A few loose rails, but I've already nailed them back in place."

Connor nodded to the herd grazing in the distance. "We can move quite a few more head into this pasture. There's enough spring foliage already and the pond is full."

"Yeah, I was thinking that as I rode out here." Caden tipped his hat back and squinted toward the late afternoon, lowering sun. "Might as well call it a day. We've got time to get cleaned up and eat before heading to the club."

Connor cut his brother a quick glance as they turned their horses back to the barns. The thought of going to The Barn held no appeal, and he knew what Caden was going to say to that. "I think I'll pass tonight. I want to check on the plans for repairing the Barton's stable." That was the excuse he planned to use for showing up at Tam's tonight. He hadn't tried to contact her all week, thinking it best if they each took the time to come to terms with the reversal of their relationship, but his need to see her in person and ensure she wouldn't pull another silent treatment could no longer be put on hold.

Caden shrugged, as if his decision was no big deal. "Sure, if that's what you want. You may as well get used to being alone, because you and I both know you won't be satisfied with anyone else."

Connor didn't have a reply to that statement as he wasn't sure his brother was wrong.

By the time he joined Caden and Sydney for dinner and then returned to his place for a shower, it was after eight when Connor pulled in front of Tam's house and saw her lit up porch. A familiar thread of excitement coursed through him as he hopped out of the truck, the same thrill he experienced every time he had showed up here to spend the night with her. He tried stifling it as he walked across the lawn toward the stable lit by outdoor floodlights, but that did little good.

The charred side of the stable had been removed and several supporting posts had been erected in its place, securing the roof. Enough progress had been made to ensure the structure's safety, but he could see the horses were still kept out in the pasture as a precaution. Satisfied they were on a steady track toward final repairs, he pivoted and started back up to the house just as Jason and Amy pulled in behind his truck. He imagined he wasn't Amy's favorite person right now, but he couldn't avoid talking to either of them as they waited outside for him.

Wondering why Tam hadn't come out, Connor strode up to greet the couple. "Evening. I just stopped by to check on the progress of the stable and talk to Tam. It looks good." He nodded toward the small barn.

"We were lucky to get a contractor out here right away to assess the damage and he'll return Monday to start putting up the NE wall," Jason replied, leaning against his truck and folding his arms across his chest as he eyed Connor with a cool gaze.

Instead of addressing that censuring look, he started to step toward the porch, but Amy halted him in his tracks with one short sentence. "She's not here."

Frowning, he whipped his eyes to her smug face. "Where is she?"

Cocking her head, she replied in a tone that indicated he should know the answer to that question. "She went to your club. You didn't expect her to sit around here just because you two split up, did you?"

Connor jerked as if struck. He never imagined Tam would return to the club without him, not after what they had shared together. How could he have forgotten the girl never behaved the way he thought she should? "I see," he returned stiffly, not liking the thought of her with someone else. *What? Did you expect her to pine away for you forever?* He hadn't thought ahead, to what she might do or whom she might turn to next. His only concern had been for her welfare and safety, like always.

Amy's face softened, and she reached out to lay a comforting hand on his rigid arm. "We both know our girl very well, Connor. It broke our hearts, Richard and I, when she accepted that job in Boise after moping around here for weeks, even though we tried to stay supportive when she first mentioned applying for it. We missed her, even though she came back a lot, it wasn't the same around here without her." She shook her head ruefully. "I venture to say she returned more during that time than you knew. She usually tells me everything, but she's kept quiet about whatever happened that prompted her to make that decision."

Connor glanced at Jason's silent, rigid stance and then back at Tam's stepmother with a resigned sigh. "I said something… hurtful, without thinking. I didn't mean it, but the damage was done, and she refused to let me apologize. But that was different. Back then, we weren't involved."

A low laugh shook Amy's shoulders. "Oh, Connor, you two have always been involved, in one form or another. She's as stubborn as you in some regards. I'm guessing something happened that made you see her in a different way, a way you weren't ready for, or didn't want. You love her. It's time you admitted that. Past time," she chided gently.

He frowned. "I've never denied I love her, Amy."

"Okay, I'll rephrase that. You're *in* love with her now." Dropping her hand, she said, "Question is, what are you going to do about it? Maybe, if you had told her you were in your new relationship for the long haul, that she wasn't just another in a long line of short affairs, she might have been more comfortable sharing her burdens with you, and you would've known what was happening. You weren't around for her in Boise, and she got along fine without you, or us. I'm sure she'll do so again."

Amy left him standing there in surprise at the cool rebuke in her tone and words, wondering if she was right. Was he as much at fault because of *his* lack of communication as he blamed her for? How could he fault Tam, and the change in their relationship he'd succumbed to for his failure to watch out for her when he was just as guilty of not being up front with her?

"I do," he called out as Amy and Jason strolled up the steps to the house.

Jason was the one who turned his head and asked, "You do, what?"

"Love her, am in love with her."

The foreman cocked an eyebrow. "Then I suggest you do something about it before you lose her again, this time for good."

Chapter 13

"Men," Nan scoffed. "Can't live with them, don't want to live without them."

Tamara sipped the beer Caden had handed her with a knowing look of support, peering at her friend over the bottle. Seated at a table with BDSM play taking place upstairs and down, the two of them had turned down several offers to play, Nan offering to stay by her side and keep her company for as long as Tamara wanted. At least she was one friend who didn't turn her back on her when confronted with feelings she didn't want to acknowledge, like someone else she was trying so hard not to think about.

"You are so right, Nan. I'm going to miss you. How long did you say you'll be gone?"

Nan grinned. "Just a few weeks. I haven't been back to New Orleans since Christmas and Jay misses me."

"How is he? Is your brother still single?" Tamara injected a teasing, hopeful note into her voice.

Laughing, Nan raised her beer in a salute. "Now you're thinking, girlfriend. Too bad Jay is now a diehard New Orleanian. We're as close as siblings can get, yet he's only made the trip to Willow Springs once to visit me since I inherited Gram's shop."

"But he grew up here with you. Doesn't he miss Willow Springs? I did when I left." Tamara remembered Nan's older brother as a good looking, friendly teen before he'd gone off to college and then settled in Louisiana, where Nan's parents had retired to before they'd both died in a car accident.

"Sure, but like a lot of young people itching to see the world beyond Montana, he left without intending to return permanently."

Tamara let her eyes wander up to the loft as she heard a strident cry, a sigh of despondency escaping her as she spotted Avery bound on the St. Andrew Cross, Master Grayson running his hands over her quivering, glistening body. "Too bad I can't take off from the new job yet, otherwise I could go with you for a few days," she stated, sliding her gaze away from the look of contented pleasure reflected on her friend's face.

Nan's frown turned fierce. "Don't you let that moron drive you away again. I swear, if you do, I'll come after both of you."

"Whoa, what or who has you showing your claws?" Master Dan asked as he, Greg and Devin strolled up to their table.

"Go away." Nan waved her hand holding the beer. "We're not doing men tonight."

"Girls? Can we watch?" Master Greg wanted to know with an eager glint in his eyes.

Tamara laughed and Nan rolled her eyes. "Sorry to disappoint you, but not girls either," Tamara quipped, liking the way the two business partners and best friends were looking at her. It helped her ego to know other men found her attractive and wanted her, even for just a few hours, and helped dispel her gloom. Her face warmed from the appreciative light in their eyes as they took in her short black skirt paired with a soft gray satin tank that draped around the shape of her braless breasts. Unfortunately, the rest of her body remained cold to the thought of baring herself for another's touch.

Dan fisted his hands on his hips and narrowed his dark chocolate eyes. "What has the two of you sitting here pouting?"

"We're not pouting, just not in the mood to play," Nan returned with a lift of one slim brow.

Tamara flicked her a quick look and saw the lust her friend always exhibited toward Master Dan. She knew the two were good friends outside the club and that he was the one Dom Nan enjoyed playing with on a regular basis. Wearing a calf-length, sheer sheath that revealed her turgid nipples and every dip of her curves, it was obvious to Tamara that Nan would be engaged in a scene with him, or someone else by now if she wasn't sitting here with her.

Feeling guilty, she nudged her with her foot under the table. "Go on, Nan. You don't need to sit here and keep me company."

"Not when we'd be happy to," Master Devin said.

Master Dan held out his hand to Nan. She took it but cast Tamara a concerned look before rising. "Are you sure?"

"Yes, go." She waved her on and Greg and Devin joined her at the table as they walked off.

Left alone with the two Doms, Tamara tried to drum up some enthusiasm for their company. Who wouldn't be thrilled with the attention of two men who could make a girl cream her panties with just a look? But if her melancholy and disinterest the past hour was any indication, the one short week Connor had indulged her craving for more of him had ruined her for anyone else, at least for the time being. Instead of admitting she wouldn't change her mind about pairing up with anyone tonight, she started to tell Master Greg and Master Devin she planned to leave early when the words lodged in her throat as Connor walked in.

With a startled jerk, Tamara's body went hot and damp with a yearning so strong it left her shaken. Tears pricked the back of her eyes as she watched him cross the room in that cocky, loose-limbed stride, wearing his usual snug jeans and the same leather vest she'd seen him in before. With all that bare, tanned skin and those bulging muscles displayed, was it any wonder he drew so many female eyes his way?

"It looks like we'll have to set our sights on another sub," Master Greg drawled, his green eyes shifting from Tamara's flushed face to Connor as he approached their table.

Master Devin cocked his head at Connor, leaning back in his chair with nonchalance as he brought his bourbon filled glass to his lips before greeting his friend. "I heard you weren't coming out tonight."

Connor shrugged and looked at Tamara. "I changed my mind when I heard my sub planned to be here." Holding out his hand, his blue eyes softened with appeal as he said, "Come with me please."

Tamara stiffened, trying her best to resist him. "Why?" she asked, stalling for time to get herself under control since they both knew she would cave.

"I'd like to tell you a story. It's a favorite of mine."

"I'm not in the mood for a story," she returned, despite the rapid beat of her heart urging her to take his hand.

"You'll like this one, I promise. Please, little one."

How did I ever think I could move on without him? It was more than physical attraction, although there was no denying the tug of those feelings. She already throbbed and he hadn't even touched her yet. With a sigh of resignation, she flicked the other two men an apologetic glance.

"Excuse me, please." As difficult as it was, she ignored Connor's outstretched hand as she stood and looked up at him. "I'll listen to your story and then I'm leaving." She wanted to stay a part of his life, but she wouldn't leave herself open to get hurt again, no matter his good intentions.

Connor nodded, rested a hand on her lower back and prodded her forward as he said, "Thanks, guys."

Without answering him, Devin told Tamara, "Look us up if you decide to stay longer."

THE URGE TO go all caveman, toss Tam… Tamara over his shoulder and take her back to his place rushed through Connor the minute he spotted her sitting with Greg and Devin. The way her pewter eyes turned wary and she'd stiffened as she looked up at him had hurt, more so because her reaction was his fault and justified. He'd been blind and resistant to change for way too long, and he prayed he wasn't too late to set things right between them.

As they reached the stairs to the loft, she paused and gave him another skeptical glance. "Why are we going upstairs if you want to talk?"

"Because I have this craving to touch you as well," he admitted honestly as he snatched her hand and tugged.

Her eyes sparked with excitement before cooling, a small sign that gave him hope. "Connor…"

"We're in the club, sweetie, so that's Master Connor." Ignoring her scowl at the endearment, he trotted upstairs and didn't pause until they reached a chain station. Reaching for the back zipper on her skirt, he began his narrative. "Once upon a time there was a cocky eighteen-year-old who had already sampled his share of girls and was looking forward to college."

Tugging the skirt down, she grasped his shoulders, snorting softly. "Let me guess. You?"

Connor pinched her bare thigh as she stepped out of the skirt. "Quiet and listen." Whipping her top over her head, he tossed it down and lifted her arms to the dangling cuffs. "One afternoon, he volunteered to assist in the riding ring at the county fair, looked up and saw the prettiest little kid struggling to hold her seat." Tam's eyes went molten as he secured her wrists and ran his hands down the underside of her arms, over her shoulders and cupped her soft breasts. She bit her lip, and he knew she wanted to resist him as much as she yearned for more of both his tale and his touch. His fragile hope just edged toward blossoming success.

"The young girl's wide eyes were filled with fear, but her small chin was rigid with fierce determination." He rasped her nipples with his thumbs, and she swayed toward him with a low moan. "He admired the young girl's grit in the face of her terror, wondered how the hell she'd reached the age of ten in ranch country without being on a horse and found himself dashing to her rescue as she lost her grip." Dipping his head, he licked over each nipple before lifting his eyes up to her flushed face. "Thus began a friendship he never imagined would grow into an obsession to see to this girl's every need, including ensuring her safety and happiness."

"C… Master Con," she breathed, her eyes softening to a silver glow. "I…"

A WICKED, teasing grin replaced Con's serious expression as he swatted right between Tamara's legs, the sudden hot pain covering her bare labia causing her to jerk in the bonds. Her thick cream spilled from her swollen lips and she didn't know what she wanted more of – his touch or his story.

Running his hands down her quivering abdomen, he slid between her thighs and cupped her throbbing pussy. "As I was saying before I was so rudely interrupted, this young man appointed himself the little girl's guardian, protector and friend." He slid two fingers inside her and her head fell back as she jutted her pelvis into his marauding hand. "He taught her to ride and jump, encouraged her to compete, sat with her family and glowed with pride when she won championships."

Tamara's body infused with heat as he slowly fingered her pussy, gliding over her clit with touches that were way too light and too short for her satisfaction. He leaned toward her close enough his chest hairs tickled her turgid nipples as he brushed her lips with his. His deep, serious voice resonated between them.

"He rescued her from randy teenage boys, helped her get through Algebra and took her for ice cream on Sunday afternoons."

Tamara smiled at the memories. "I remember…"

He laid a finger damp with her juices over her mouth. "Shh, almost done." Rubbing the wetness across her lips, he said, "And then, one day she looked at him with the lust of a young woman, a look that caught him by surprise and that he tried to ignore because she was still too young for his tastes and she was the kid next door, not someone to be dallied with."

Tamara watched him retrieve a condom from his pocket, shuffling her feet apart in anticipation of the wonderful stretch and burn of his cock surging inside her again. Had it really only been a week since he'd taken her last? As much as she loved his story and the new light of acceptance shining in his eyes, she was dying for his rough possession right now more than anything else.

"Where… where are you going with this tale?" she gasped, unable to resist prodding him along.

"To that day five years ago when this arrogant man made the biggest mistake of his life."

"What… what mistake was that?" she moaned as he grasped her buttocks and worked his rigid erection inside her pussy one excruciating slow inch at a time.

"He drove away the girl he had sworn to always protect and be there for, and why?" Pulling back, he thrust into her with a forceful plunge. "Because he'd fallen in love and it scared the hell out of him. Then he realized something tonight."

Tears filled Tamara's eyes as she looked into his face, his bristled jaw taut with hunger, his eyes soft with the love he'd just admitted to. "What?"

Connor squeezed her buttocks as he dragged his flesh over her sensitive, swollen tissues. "That what better way to watch over her was to be right," he pulled back then thrust forward again, "here, all the time."

Tamara cried out with the next ramming stroke. "Oh God, Con, what the hell took you so long?"

With a laugh of sheer pleasure, Connor drove her to the heights of ecstasy only he could, bright lights exploding behind her closed eyes promising a wonderful future ahead for them. She was still panting, her sweat-slick body shuddering as he released her, and she fell into his arms.

"I've got you, sweetie."

Peering up at his crooked grin, she cupped his face, saying, "Con, I love you with all my heart, but don't call me sweetie."

"Not even if you're my only girl from now on?"

"Oh, well, if you put it like that."

THE END

BJ Wane

I live in the Midwest with my husband and our two dogs, a Poodle/Pyrenees mix and an Irish Water Spaniel. I love dogs, spending time with my daughter, babysitting her two dogs, reading and working puzzles. We have traveled extensively throughout the states, Canada and just once overseas, but I much prefer being a homebody. I worked for a while writing articles for a local magazine but soon found my interest in writing for myself peaking. My first book was strictly spanking erotica, but I slowly evolved to writing erotic romance with an emphasis on spanking. I love hearing from readers and can be reached here: bjwane@cox.net.

Recent accolades include: 5 star, Top Pick review from The Romance Reviews for *Blindsided*, 5 star review from Long & Short Reviews for Hannah & The Dom Next Door, which was also voted Erotic Romance of the Month on LASR, and my most recent title, Her Master At Last, took two spots on top 100 lists in BDSM erotica and Romantic erotica in less than a week!

Visit her Facebook page
https://www.facebook.com/bj.wane
Visit her blog here
bjwane.blogspot.com

Don't miss these exciting titles by BJ Wane and Blushing Books!

Single Titles
Claiming Mia

Cowboy Doms Series
Submitting to the Rancher, Book 1
Submitting to the Sheriff, Book 2
Submitting to the Cowboy, Book 3

Virginia Bluebloods Series
Blindsided, Book 1
Bind Me To You, Book 2
Surrender To Me, Book 3
Blackmailed, Book 4
Bound By Two, Book 5
Determined to Master: Complete Series

Murder On Magnolia Island:
The Complete Trilogy
Logan - Book 1
Hunter - Book 2
Ryder - Book 3

Miami Masters
Bound and Saved - Book One
Master Me, Please - Book Two
Mastering Her Fear - Book Three
Bound to Submit - Book Four
His to Master and Own - Book Five
Theirs to Master - Book Six

Masters of the Castle
Witness Protection Program
(Controlling Carlie)

Connect with BJ Wane
bjwane.blogspot.com